Go To Hail

Book 2 of The Hail Raisers

By

Lani Lynn Vale

**ISBN-13:
978-1978424258**

**ISBN-10:
1978424256**

Dedication

To my son, who right now is outside my window shooting a bow and arrow at a target that makes a shit ton of noise. I love you, but right now, you're driving me insane so this one is to you. <3

Acknowledgements

Kellie Montgomery- Thank you for reading these, and never complaining about the amount of crap you have to fix.

Ellie McLove- Thank you so much for agreeing to take me on as an editor. I hope you don’t regret it. LOL

Golden Czermak- I love that you do what you do. You certainly make my life a whole lot easier when it comes to finding the perfect cover for my babies.

Andrew James- your picture blew me away. Thank you for posing for it!

CONTENTS

Other titles by Lani Lynn Vale:

The Freebirds

Boomtown

Highway Don't Care

Another One Bites the Dust

Last Day of My Life

Texas Tornado

I Don't Dance

The Heroes of The Dixie Wardens MC

Lights To My Siren

Halligan To My Axe

Kevlar To My Vest

Keys To My Cuffs

Life To My Flight

Charge To My Line

Counter To My Intelligence

Right To My Wrong

Code 11- KPD SWAT

Center Mass

Double Tap

Bang Switch

Execution Style

Charlie Foxtrot

Kill Shot

Coup De Grace

The Uncertain Saints

Whiskey Neat

Jack & Coke

Go to Hail

Vodka On The Rocks

Bad Apple

Dirty Mother

Rusty Nail

The Kilgore Fire Series

Shock Advised

Flash Point

Oxygen Deprived

Controlled Burn

Put Out

I Like Big Dragons Series

I Like Big Dragons and I Cannot Lie

Dragons Need Love, Too

Oh, My Dragon

The Dixie Warden Rejects

Beard Mode

Fear the Beard

Son of a Beard

I'm Only Here for the Beard

The Beard Made Me Do It

Beard Up

For the Love of Beard

There's No Crying in Baseball

Pitch Please

The Hail Raisers

Hail No

Go to Hail

PROLOGUE

Life is so boring when you don't have an online order to look forward to.
-Fact of Life

Travis

I watched her cross the room, and I liked what I saw.

My breath caught in my throat, and my heart started to pound.

That was unusual.

Normally, I tried to stay away from women.

They were trouble.

Big fucking trouble.

Trouble that I didn't have time to deal with right then.

"… she's one of my good friends who is here to help ascertain if any of these ladies are in need of medical attention. Hannah, this is Travis Hail. Do you…"

Her name. He'd said her name. *What was her name?*

He'd said something more, but I couldn't fucking breathe.

This close, she was goddamn mesmerizing.

We stared into each other's eyes long enough to acknowledge that there was something there, but moments later a pained cry from a woman across the room had Hannah whirling around like she'd been called directly by name.

Then she was gone, and I watched her work.

Watched while she did her job, and made sure that every person that she was helping had the best possible care she could give.

Then, as if in a daze, she disappeared once everything was said and done.

And I was left wondering who the hell the girl was that had made my heart sing.

CHAPTER 1

I want to be a nice person, but everyone is just so stupid.
-Travis' secret thoughts

Travis

I looked around the house, wondering how this had become my life.

Seven years ago, everything was okay.

Seven years ago, I was living the dream.

I had my own business that my brother and I had purchased with help from my father. Dante was my partner. We opened a club together. I had a wife and kid.

And now…*nothing.*

My wife was no more. I had a kid that hated me because her mother poisoned everything that came out of her mouth.

And, now there was Dante who was so far in the deep end, head barely above water, that I wasn't sure whether he was going to sink or swim.

I was short a few drivers at our business, working fourteen-hour days at minimum. I needed at least three more workers and about ten more hours in the day to cover the workload that Dante had left behind.

And then there was Hannah…and my son, Travis Junior, also known as TJ.

“Anything?”

I looked over to find my other brother, Reed, standing in the doorway.

“He’s gone,” I said, sounding as tired as I felt. “Either he took my advice to heart, or he got out of here before I could give him any more of my recommendations.”

Reed grunted something.

“You need to give him time.”

I looked over to find my other brother, Baylor, standing there. He had a white piece of paper in his hands, and he was holding it out to me.

“I’ve given him time, Baylor,” I told him, taking the paper. “We’ve all given him time. Hell, I know he needs more time, but I can’t do this on my own. I know y’all are helping, and it’s nice. But he’s co-owner of this business with me. I can’t do anything without his consent. It’s the law…”

I trailed off as I got the first look at the paper he’d handed me, and the moment I saw it, my heart sank to around my knees.

“No.”

The word was pulled from the deepest part of my belly, and so angry and upset that it was a wonder that the walls of Dante’s house didn’t crumble around me.

“You need to give him time,” Baylor repeated.

I looked up at the huge floor to ceiling fireplace. It was gorgeous. Made of rough cut stone, it was something that I remembered Dante and his dead wife building to this day.

It'd been something to see, because his wife could barely even lift up the rocks as she handed them to him.

In the center of that fireplace was a photograph of Dante's family. His wife. His two kids. Him.

They all looked so fuckin' happy.

There was no way for them to know that a mere week after taking that picture, they would all die in a car crash caused by our very own sister.

That Dante would have to listen to his wife and two kids scream in panic until the line went dead and the car fully submerged while he sat in the tow truck next to me, alive and well.

"Tobias found the woman."

We all knew the woman that Reed was talking about. The woman was a woman that Dante had slept with. Once he'd done the deed, he'd said words, she'd packed up, and he'd gone back to the falling apart man that we were left with after his wife and kids were killed. Only, he hadn't realized that he left a little piece of himself behind in the woman.

"Well, maybe that'll be the lifeboat in this sinking ship of a life we have," Baylor murmured. Then, the words we weren't meant to hear, came. "But I doubt it."

"Let's go," I said, looking away from the photo. "With this, I might be able to get shit done and remain out of jail. But I don't think this is the end. This is only the beginning."

***

Four hours later, I walked into the house.

Hannah and her daughter, Reggie, from a previous relationship, were on the floor putting a large puzzle together.

The second I came through the door, Reggie was up and running at my legs.

"Hey there, girly girl," I murmured to the little tot that looked so much like her mother that it hurt. "How are you doing tonight?"

Reggie was an eight-year-old bundle of energy that was the absolute cutest thing that I'd ever seen in my life. And that was saying something because I had some cute kids.

TJ was all me, from the top of his curly-haired head to the bottom of his long toes. My other daughter, Alexandra, from my first marriage, was also my mini-me, only in female form. She had beautiful long curly hair, piercing eyes exactly like mine, and skin the color of mocha chocolate, thanks to her Puerto Rican mother's heritage.

But Reggie?

God, she was all Hannah. Long, curly blonde hair, bright blue eyes, skin that always had a slight tan. She was literally what you would think about when you thought of a beautiful child.

There was no doubt in my mind that she would grow up to be a breathtaking adult.

And when that day came, my heart would literally ache.

"I made a one hundred on my sight words," she declared. "And I can read like Mama!"

I looked over to Hannah, who was staring down at the puzzle instead of looking at me, and my heart squeezed.

God, I was ruining everyone's lives.

I didn't know what to do!

I was stuck…and it was all Allegra Levaux's fault.

"Maybe you can read to me instead of me reading to you tonight."

Reggie's face lit up with wonder. "I can do that?"

I started to chuckle and then dropped a kiss onto her head.

"Yeah, baby. We can do that." I winked at her, and she giggled.

"Come help me and Mama finish this puzzle," she ordered. "It's a five hundred piece one of Elsa. Mama says she hates them."

I knew she hated puzzles.

I was a puzzle.

One she couldn't figure out.

The only problem was that there was no puzzle to figure out. I knew what was wrong with me.

She knew what was wrong with me.

It was something that I couldn't fix…not and continue seeing my other kid.

Allegra, my other child's mother, was a vindictive bitch.

The moment I met Hannah, she'd started turning Alex against me.

What had once been my baby girl, my mini-me in everything that I did, now hated my guts.

And there was nothing I could do to stop it.

Either I left Hannah and TJ, or I didn't get to see Alex.

It was a lose-lose situation. One that I wasn't sure that I could ever possibly win.

"I can help," I offered, walking to the back of the couch and placing my hand on the back to steady myself. "Just let me get my boots off."

They were covered in grease and grime from the shop.

One of our new trucks had been damaged during a call, and I'd had to help fix it up to get it back into service.

It'd taken an hour out of my approved time with Alex, and at this point, I couldn't say that it was bothering me.

There was only so much you could take of your daughter saying she hated you before you believed her.

Walking into Reggie's warming embrace was like summer compared to Alex's winter.

You'd never be able to tell that Alex and Reggie were the same age.

Alex was quiet, withdrawn, and quick to rile.

Reggie was loud, rambunctious, and never met a stranger.

They were both eight years old, and neither one of them had their father in their lives.

Though, that wasn't my doing on Alex's part.

I tried to have a place in her life. Even though the last year Alex had done nothing but spew nasty words at me the entire time she was with me, I still picked her up on Wednesdays and took her out to eat. I still picked her up on the weekends and took her to Dante's place to spend the weekend with her.

I couldn't take her home, though.

Hannah, Reggie, and TJ were in my home.

We may not be together, Hannah and I, but we *were* a family.

I wanted Hannah more than my next breath, but with Allegra's threats, and Alex's proof that she wasn't threatening me, I didn't have much I could do.

So Hannah was just my roommate.

Hell, I was barely ever here.

TJ was now two months old, and in daycare because both of his parents worked.

I wanted to be able to give my child the time and devotion I'd shown Alex when she'd been a baby, but at this point in my life, it just wasn't feasible.

An hour after I put TJ to bed, Hannah stopped by the couch with an armful of laundry and asked me what I knew she would ask me.

"How did your night with Alex go?"

I looked up from the paperwork that I was filling out at the coffee table and saw her beautiful eyes on me.

God, it was like a shot straight to the heart.

"She said she hated me no less than a hundred times. Screamed that I was hurting her while we were out having pizza, and told some lady that I'd kidnapped her."

Hannah's mouth fell open in shock.

"You're joking."

I closed my eyes, dropped my pen, and let the remembrance of the hellish night sweep through me.

"No, not kidding at all," I moaned into my hands. "I guess I'm just lucky that the police department is still under construction."

Two months ago, corruption had been discovered in our local police department, and it'd been shut down pending further investigation. A month ago, the choice to reopen, but hold an election for the chief of police, had been decided. They'd also concluded that everyone in the department was being terminated, even the ones that weren't convicted of any wrongdoing. They'd sat idly by and let whatever happened, happen.

The next Chief of Police would be the one to choose his staff.

The election had been a week ago, and the new chief was building his department. It took time, though, and thank God for that.

"What happened?"

Hannah dropped the clothes on the back of the couch and circled it, stopping beside the chair that was at an angle to the couch, and planted herself in it.

I tried not to watch the way her shorts rode up her thighs, or the way her breasts that were full of milk for our child practically spilled out of her shirt.

She wasn't wearing a bra, either.

I swallowed and looked back down at the coffee table.

All the numbers that I was crunching were blurring together.

"The lady at the counter that had checked us out knew me. Knew that Alex was my child." I sighed. "Since she's the owner, everyone was a whole lot more forgiving. Plus, you know how Tanny is. She's so freakin' grandmotherly that nobody would dare challenge her word."

Hannah's mouth twitched, but just as quickly, that humor fled.

"You need to do something here, Travis."

I knew it.

She knew it.

We all fucking knew it.

I just didn't know *what* to do.

"I don't know how to fix this," I admitted. "I'm literally hanging on, doing everything I can, but it's never enough."

She didn't come to me. Didn't put her hands on me. Didn't even twitch.

God, I wanted that so badly.

But Allegra had already proven that she would do just about anything to keep me exactly how she wanted me.

If there was an award for most awful ex-wife, Allegra would win it twice.

She didn't want me. She divorced me a year after Alex was born, and that was a shocker.

I'd thought that everything was going great. Sure, I was a distracted man at times since I was helping grow a business with Dante, but I was still home every night by five, home on the weekends. She had a nice house, good clothes covering her back, and a cleaning lady that came in once a week to make sure Allegra didn't have to stress herself.

Then, one day out of the blue, she'd decided to leave.

There'd been no convincing her to stay, and I'd been left feeling incredibly confused.

Alex had been, too.

And for her, I'd decided that the best thing to do was not to fight it. To get our lives back to normal—or as normal as two adults and a child could be when they were no longer a family—and make sure that Alex never wanted for anything. But she did that staying with her mother.

We'd worked out a visitation schedule without lawyers. We'd split as amicably as a man could when he didn't want to leave his wife, and things had become our new normal.

Only Allegra was a bitch. This I found out over the next seven years as I started to get out in the world. To be happy again.

The moment that I slept with my first woman after Allegra, Alex missed her first Wednesday visitation with me. Because Allegra, supposedly, 'forgot.'

It only got worse after that.

CHAPTER 2

I'm skipping the gym today because I already have a six-pack. At home. In the fridge.
-Things you probably shouldn't say to your personal trainer

Travis

I woke up the next morning, my eyes heavy with sleep.

TJ hadn't had a good night, and since Hannah had

to go back to work tomorrow, I volunteered to help.

The problem was that the only thing I could really help with at this point was going to get him, changing his diaper, and handing him over.

Yesterday, she'd started pumping for him to have his meals at daycare. But I couldn't feed him those in the middle of the night, otherwise he wouldn't have any to eat while Hannah was gone during the day.

Hence why I'd only done the easy things and then handed him over.

When I'd walked into her room in the middle of the night with TJ in my arms, I'd frozen to the spot.

She wore nothing but a t-shirt and panties.

Her breasts were unbound, and they were pressing against the t-shirt (my t-shirt that she'd stolen when she'd gotten too pregnant to wear anything else but my shirts and her scrubs) with delicious intent.

I'd barely had the heart to wake her, but since TJ had started crying, effectively putting an end to anything I'd wanted, it hadn't mattered.

"Do you know what I'm putting on my pancakes?" Reggie whispered conspiratorially in my ear.

I grinned and opened my eyes, rolling just my head on the pillow to see Reggie within inches of my face.

"No," I rumbled, voice thick with sleep. "What?"

Had Hannah made a feast that I wasn't aware of? Damn, that sure did sound nice.

Normally, though, Hannah only had time for the frozen silver dollar sized pancakes that came in packages of one hundred from the store. Though, that was more than Alex had gotten when Allegra was running late and in charge of breakfast. When it was up to her, she drove Alex by Sonic or McDonald's, got her a biscuit sandwich, and called it good.

At least Hannah fed her kid at home.

"Syrup."

I burst out laughing.

"Oh, yeah?" I asked. "What's the big secret?"

She grinned. "Mama warmed it up in the microwave, first. Did you know, that on the new bottle, they have a little microwave window that tells you when it's at the perfect temperature?"

I did, but I acted like it was the newest invention since sliced bread.

"No, really?"

I pushed up to my ass and slid my feet over the side of the bed, only then realizing that I was in my underwear.

Shit.

I tried really hard not to be caught so indecent in front of Reggie.

I didn't want to give my ex-fucking-wife *any* reason to call the cops. *Again.*

Bitch.

I didn't know how Allegra found out the stuff she did. I didn't know who she had working in her pocket at the police station—although thank God that was no longer a factor—but she always seemed to find a way to fuck me over.

She had to have eyes everywhere, and I was halfway convinced that she was spying on me in my own place of business.

"Mama said to let you sleep," Reggie continued, not noticing anything of my discomfort.

I leaned down and snatched up the sheet that'd been knocked to the floor sometime in between three in the morning and now, which was a little past six. The moment I had it around my waist, I walked into the attached bathroom and closed the door, immediately yanking on the pair of sweats that'd been there from my run the day before.

The moment I was dressed, I walked back out into my room to find Reggie on her belly, her face buried in my pillow, sound asleep.

I blinked.

Literally, the kid could fall asleep anywhere.

I envied her that.

"Is there anything you want me to get at the store tonight?" Hannah asked hesitantly.

I whirled to find her standing in the doorway.

Goddammit. I really hated that she was so fucking cautious around me now.

She wasn't sure what to say. Hell, half the time I expected to come to the house and find her packed up and gone.

I felt like an utter ass.

What I wouldn't give to have her back to the way I first met her.

CHAPTER 3

Just once in my life, I'd actually like to see a liar's pants catch on fire.
-Coffee Cup

Hannah

389 days ago

"Hello?" I answered, walking toward my car with Reggie holding onto my hand, trotting along behind me.

"You get settled in yet?"

I smiled as I looked at the door to my place.

"Yes, we're settled…why?"

"Because," I heard through both my phone and in front of me, "I'm here, and I want to make sure I'm not about to be sent away again when I've just driven two hours to see my niece."

I looked up and immediately smiled at my brother.

"Hey, Michael," I grinned.

"Uncle Mikey!" came my seven-year old's screeched squeal. "You're here!"

Michael shoved his phone into his pocket and took the stairs two at a time, making it three-quarters of the way down before Reggie hit him like a tiny little land piranha.

My brother scooped her up into his arms, buried his face into my girl's neck, and pretended to eat her.

Reggie, of course, shrieked in glee.

She loved her Uncle Mikey with everything she had, and the day I took her away from him and moved to Uncertain, and then to Hostel from there, was the day that I 'ruined her life.' Or so she said, anyway.

She quickly forgot, but she didn't forget how much she loved her uncle.

"You want to come eat dinner with me and watch a movie, Monster?" Michael asked her.

My lips tipped up at the corners.

"What kind of silly question is that?" my daughter shot back. "Of course, I do!"

"You don't think your momma will care if I steal you away?"

God, please take her! my eyes said pleadingly.

My daughter was a beautiful, intelligent, delight of a child.

But, she was also a handful.

Beautiful, intelligent children who had an IQ as high as Reggie's needed stimulation. My brain was tired.

It would be nice to get a few minutes peace and quiet.

My daughter looked at me pleadingly, and I changed my expression to one of contemplation.

"Mama!"

I rolled my eyes skyward and sighed.

“I think that she said yes.”

I laughed. “You would think that, wouldn’t you, Mikey?”

He winked at me, came down the rest of the stairs, and then threw his arm around my shoulder.

“I’ve missed you, sis.”

I closed my eyes and rubbed my face on his tattooed forearm.

“I love you, too, Mikey.”

Mikey didn’t do the sweetness all that often, but when he did, I savored it.

He was a badass SWAT officer. If he acted like he was a big ol’ teddy bear, then his reputation would be ruined.

Or so he said.

“Whatever,” he grumbled. “Go out. Get some food. Have some fun. Do what you said your co-worker asked you to do today.”

I snorted.

I was not going to a club and ‘unwinding’ with the sluttiest co-worker that Jefferson had to offer. It just wasn’t happening.

***

Three hours later, I was a little bit tipsy, and watching the most handsome man in the world from across the bar.

God, he was eye-catching.

He had the build of a runner. All wiry and lean. Though, that didn’t mean he didn’t have muscles, because he did. Those arms were to die for, and the tattoos? Those only made those muscles even better.

From across the bar, I couldn't see what the tattoos looked like, but I wasn't sure if it'd matter—as long as it didn't say some long-lost love's name, I was pretty okay with any tattoo!

He was wearing faded blue jeans, a gray t-shirt with 'Hail Auto Recovery' on the back of it in white vinyl letters. Underneath the lettering was a picture of a tow-truck…one that resembled the six tow trucks that I'd parked beside after pulling into the parking lot earlier.

Apparently, the entire Hail Auto Recovery crew was here unwinding after a long day of work.

Kind of like I was.

"Hey!" Wednesday cried out. "Are you going to drink that?"

I looked at the beer I'd been nursing for the last half an hour and shook my head.

"I was going to, but it's warm now. Do you want it?" I asked, offering her the mug. "I was about to go get a refill."

As long as the hottie at the bar moved.

I couldn't walk up and ask the bartender for another beer with him sitting there. There was no way that I'd manage to do it.

I'd either A, walk up and trip, smacking my face on his barstool, or B, spill my beer on either him or myself. Both of which I'd done before.

I was what you would call an awkward woman.

I was an introvert, and on top of that, I found it hard to talk to anyone that wasn't coming to see me in a medical capacity.

Why I could talk to patients all day long, and not talk to a man that was at a bar, I had no idea. But I couldn't, and I'd long since decided that it was going to forever be that way.

I'd come to terms with that fact a long time ago...right along the time that I met my ex-husband.

A man that was almost as awkward as me, and quickly made me realize that I was just different.

Except, Joshua, my ex-husband, didn't really think that. He thought I was odd, and that I'd get over my strangeness once I grew older.

When I didn't and made an embarrassment of myself and him at a company party (his words not mine), he decided that it was time for him to leave and make it official with his co-worker, Mandy.

Mandy, the woman that I'd cooked dinner for at my home. Mandy, the woman that watched my kid. Mandy, the woman that was also allergic to dogs, and didn't like Mogley—our dog, that we were forced to put him away while she was over.

Mandy, the whore that had been seeing him on the sly for eight months before he admitted to me that I was no longer 'his one.'

"Thanks!" Wednesday took the beer and brought it to her lips. "I can't believe I forgot my wallet!"

I could.

Wednesday was always forgetting everything.

She was a good girl and a great nurse…but with her everyday life? She was the epitome of ditzy.

She was what every blonde joke was made up of.

Poor girl.

She gave the regular blondes like me a bad rap.

I watched her chug the beer, and then slam the cup down on the table, drawing the attention of not just those around me, but also those *not* around me.

I.e., the hot guy at the bar who hadn't looked this way all night.

"I love beer!"

I would've laughed. Really, I would have, but the man's eyes were on me.

They were enthralling.

I couldn't look away and likely wouldn't have, had Wednesday not thrown herself around me and pulled me bodily to the dance floor.

Slightly tipsy or not, there was no way in hell I was going to dance with her.

I saw how she danced—and that was uninhibited. There was no way that I'd be dancing around her, not with the way she'd garnered every single man's attention tonight. And yes, that included the hot one that I was staring at for most of it.

"No," I shook off her hand. "I gotta pee!"

And hopefully find a way to get another beer without hot guy being near.

"Okay!" Wednesday chirped. "Do you want me to save you a spot?"

Save me a spot? *On the dance floor? How, exactly, would she do a thing like that?*

Dance around in a bigger circle?

"No," I tried not to laugh. "I'll catch you when you get back to the table."

"Okay," she cheered and clapped her hands. "Sounds good!"

I rolled my eyes and made my way to the bathroom, wondering why the hell I'd agreed to come with Wednesday in the first place. Likely, it was due to the fact that she bothered me relentlessly about it, and I always had an excuse.

That, and she'd met me at the grocery store after Michael had taken Reggie, and I'd not had her with me to use for an excuse. After learning that I was child-free, she had invited me out and I wasn't able to come up with an excuse fast enough and was forced to bend to her will.

Which sucked, because to be honest, it would've been incredible to have a few hours to myself without my daughter around. A bottle of wine and the last season of Blue Bloods sounded fantastic after a day like today.

As I got to the line for the women's restroom, I pulled out my phone and started to read a book.

I'd made it about a chapter and a half in before it was my turn, and only when I was about to head inside, did I look up.

I blinked when I saw the man—the hot guy—standing across the hallway from me, staring.

The hot guy that I realized that I knew now that I saw him up close and personal instead of from across a smoky, dark bar. The one man that had watched over me—thanks to Wolf's insistence—when a call for all medical personnel in the area had gone out months ago.

We hadn't spoken then. There hadn't been enough time. And when there had been time, he'd been gone.

For the life of me I couldn't remember his name, though. I'd been so enamored with meeting the man in person—I'd seen him around town quite a bit—that I'd momentarily blanked out.

When I'd come to, with my friend leaving me, he'd nodded his head at me and I'd gone to work at hearing a woman's pained cry.

"You enjoying that book?" he asked casually.

I cleared my throat, nodded, and—like the introvert that I was—walked into the bathroom and slammed the door.

"Shit!" I cursed, loudly enough for the woman at the sink to look at me.

"Sorry," I apologized for my cursing. "Stubbed my toe."

She looked down at the dusty cowboy boots I had on with my jeans, and 'hmmed' at me.

I chose to go into the bathroom stall before I said or did anything else stupid and embarrassing.

Once I was finished, I walked to the counter and washed my hands, inspecting my face.

I had a zit on the bottom of my chin. It was the size of Atlanta.

It hurt like a mother, and I was wondering if anybody beside me could see it. With the way it was positioned, I was fairly sure that nobody could, but that didn't stop me from covering it by keeping my eyes pointed at the ground as I exited.

Though that likely had a lot to do with the fact that there might be the man out in the hallway again, and I really didn't want him to see the zit that hopefully only I could see. If, on the off chance, he was still leaning against that wall.

But, the moment I arrived in the hallway, I glanced up slightly to study the area and was disappointed to find that the only people there were the women waiting in the line for the bathroom.

Shit.

But then, as I passed an open doorway, I froze when I heard that voice say, "Gonna wait right here for her."

I sped up, completely saddened to hear that my hot guy was waiting for another woman.

God, why was I so stupid?

I was a single mother. I had extra weight in my ass and thighs. I had long blonde hair, and at this point, I only had a double chin when I looked down at my iPhone. I wasn't anyone to write home about.

At least, I didn't think so.

The guy that I'd been staring at all night? *He was too hot for me.*

I was a six on the attractiveness scale. He was an eleven.

Those two didn't mix.

Not from what I could tell, anyway.

But, as I hurried past the open doorway and into the main part of the bar, I could hear hurried boot steps behind me.

The one good thing I could say about hot guy being in the back was that now the bar was free.

And now I could get that glass of wine—wine that I'd been dreaming about since this afternoon when Reggie threw a fit because I wouldn't take her to the zoo.

Maybe I could drink it, and then convince Wednesday that I had to go.

It was eight thirty. That was about an hour away from my usual bedtime, and it would be so nice to be at home and get a good night's sleep, and then not have to take Reggie to school in the morning.

On my day off.

God, I could practically feel my bed calling for me, which made me hesitate halfway to the bar. Which in turn made the man that was following at my back, catch me.

And he caught me—literally and figuratively.

How did he do that, you ask?

Due to my abrupt stop, and his hurried footsteps to keep up with me, it caused him to slam into my back.

My arms shot out to catch my fall that I knew was inevitable, but before my face could make an introduction with the floor, large arms looped around my waist and caught me.

Which then led to me bent over at the waist, his groin pressed against my ass, in the middle of the dance floor, during a song that had nearly everyone in the entire place slow dancing.

I stood up, my non-existent abs burning, and turned, staring at the man that was still holding on to me with stunned silence.

"You okay?" he questioned.

His breath smelled like whiskey.

It wasn't a bad smell, per se, but it wasn't my favorite.

But, the rest of him? He smelled like leather, a hint of grease, and man.

And his eyes were a stunning ice blue.

"Yeah?"

My yeah came out as a question, causing his hands to tighten slightly on my hips—hands that he still had firmly locked into place.

"You're not sure?"

I shrugged and then tried to pull away.

What did he do when I did? Put both of his arms around me...and then start to sway to the music.

Sway. To. The. Music.

He started dancing.

With me.

Me and my two left feet.

"Uhhh," I said, trying not to enjoy the way his hips were swaying back and forth across my pelvis. "What are you doing?"

"I was going to ask you if you wanted to have a drink with me, but dancing works, too."

I didn't know what to say to that, and so, like a fool, I stood there for a few long seconds.

And in those seconds, he took it as consent and continued to dance. This time, he smoothed one hand up my side and then down my arm, latching onto my hand.

The other moved to curve around my hip, hauling me impossibly closer.

By this point, I was on the verge of panic.

What did I do?

I stepped on his foot.

Though, not on purpose.

"I'm sorry," I apologized, pushing slightly on his arm. "I don't dance well."

"Well," he started to let me go, and the feeling of panic started to subside. "I do. So that's a win for you."

Then he spun me around like those men did to the ladies on *Dancing With The Stars*, and I gasped.

When I found myself facing the right way again, he used his hand on my hip to turn me slightly, and then he did another really cool move that had me facing away from him for a few seconds before I was turned back the right way.

I gasped, breathless, and stared at him in shock.

"What are we…"

He leaned forward, and I leaned back.

That was about when I found myself leaning backward, staring at the world upside down.

It went on like that for a few minutes longer as the song finished, and by the time he was finished, I was smiling.

"That was fun." I patted him on the shoulder and turned to walk away.

He let me go, but only long enough for me to step away and start in the direction of the door.

However, he steered me toward the bar and flagged down the bartender.

"What do you want to drink?" he asked.

A lot of wine, I mentally retorted. Audibly, I said, "Water."

The man at my side grunted something that sounded a lot like a rumbling laugh, but I didn't turn to study his face to confirm.

I kept my eyes forward and wondered if I could manage to sit on one of the bar stools without falling.

Deciding that I could likely manage it, I sat, and then immediately cursed myself.

I could feel the cool air on my exposed back and wondered again why I'd decided to wear the tank top.

"Have you ever been to Gas Monkey before?"

I blinked, turning to him as I began to tug on my shirt.

"What?" I asked in confusion.

He gestured with his head toward my breast, and my eyes followed his.

The tank top I was wearing was one that my brother had gotten me. It'd fit PR—pre-Reggie. Last week had been the first time I'd tried it on since then, and I was happy to find out that it fit, though still a little tight. It'd been one of my favorites way back when.

"Yes," I told him. "Once. Before they were popular on the TV series, though."

His brows went up.

"You watch Gas Monkey on TV?"

I nodded, then immediately thanked the bartender for my glass of water. "Yeah."

"Christ, you might very well be every man's dream girl."

When my startled eyes found his, I realized that he was staring at my ass.

I cleared my throat of embarrassment.

"W-why is that?"

I didn't know why I was every man's dream girl—at least in his way of thinking. Joshua, my ex, would beg to differ.

"You drink beer. You wear jeans so tight that I can admire your curves. You watch my favorite show…and you're fucking hot."

I found myself grinning.

"And, since I've been watching you all night, you haven't said yes to a single man when he asked you to dance."

He'd been watching me all night? He thought I was hot? Holy shit!

"Not to mention, when you felt yourself getting tipsy, you slowed down on the beer and didn't make a fool of yourself like your friend did."

I took that moment to scan the area for Wednesday, and found her standing on the edge of the dance floor, head thrown back, drinking a drink that someone had to buy for her. Hopefully she at least took it straight from the bartender.

The man that was standing next to her looked ready to pounce, and my eyes narrowed.

Wednesday had been shrugging him off all night, and she'd even told him that she didn't want to dance with him.

Why all of a sudden would she talk—let alone laugh—with him?

But, my eyes were pulled back toward Travis when he said, "What else do you like to do?"

So, that was how, over the next half hour, we talked about anything and everything. In the middle of a bar.

"What's your favorite drink?" I queried.

He snorted. "Dr. Pepper. Is there anything else to drink in Texas?"

I stuck my tongue out at him.

"Mine is Mountain Dew."

He gasped, sounding like he was highly offended by my admission.

"Blasphemy." His eyes sparkled. "I'll have to rethink this 'liking you' business."

I giggled.

Like a teenage girl.

Jesus Christ.

But before I could reply, Travis' eyebrows snapped together, and his eyes narrowed on something that was over my left shoulder.

In reaction, I turned and stared at where his gaze was pointing, and immediately got to my feet and headed in the direction of where I'd just seen Wednesday leave with the guy.

Her head had been leaning on his shoulder, and his arm was around her waist, guiding her out of the club.

That was *not* Wednesday.

Wednesday could handle her drinks. I'd once seen her down half a bottle of vodka, drink two beers, and then finish off the rest of the vodka all within a two-hour timeframe. Not once had I seen her act drunk.

How she could handle all that and still act halfway sane—and I say half because she's always partially insane—was beyond me. But the girl could do it.

I'd seen it happen.

My feet carried me outside, and before I knew it, I was scanning the parking lot for my friend.

I didn't see the familiar blonde hair, and I also didn't see Wednesday's flaming red dress.

I did hear a man talking, though, and decided that maybe I should go over to where I could hear him and ask if he'd seen her.

My first step around the side of the building had me coming face to face with the same man holding up a clearly under-the-influence Wednesday on the seat of a motorcycle—who had her skirt hiked up around her waist, with a man's face buried between her cleavage.

I snapped.

"Hey!" I screamed. "What are you doing?"

The man sneered and stood up fully, and Wednesday started to teeter off of the bike.

Her eyes were almost all the way closed, and she didn't say a word as the man caught her before she could face plant.

Thank God.

What I was not happy about, though, was the way the man was so clearly hanging onto her.

"Did you slip something into her drink?" I accused as I rushed forward.

"No," the man lied. "She's lit."

I highly doubted that.

"All right, well you can put her into my car, then," I gestured toward my car in the middle of the parking lot.

The man didn't even bother looking. Instead, he growled something.

"She's coming home with me."

I shook my head almost immediately. "No. She is not."

He fisted his hand. "And how, exactly, are you going to stop me?"

That was when Travis sidled up, surprising not just the man, but me as well.

I hadn't realized that he'd followed me out here.

Travis was not the type of man to stay silent and let a woman do the talking.

At least, I didn't think that he was.

But then I saw the other man come up at my side and realized why he hadn't immediately followed me out. He was getting backup.

Smart man.

"How about you leave before you make a scene."

And that was when, instead of helping her down nicely, the man practically shoved Wednesday off his bike.

Her entire body hit the concrete before any of us could move, and her head bounced off with sickening force.

Travis moved.

One second, he was at my side. The next, he was across the short alley and slamming his fist into the man's jaw.

The man went down hard, knocked out so quick and fast that not even he saw it coming.

Travis stood over the man with an angry expression on his face, and the man at my side whistled through his teeth.

"Damn, bro," the man at my side said. "Anger issues?"

But the 'bro' was already moving toward Wednesday.

"Careful with her head, Baylor. She may need a doctor."

I agreed but walked over to Wednesday who was rolling up to sit on her butt. When I got to her, I pulled out my phone and flipped on the flashlight, shining it into her eyes.

"Both pupils are dilated," I murmured. "She's been drugged."

I felt the back of Wednesday's head with both hands, happy when I didn't find any lumps from her fall.

Before I could help her anymore, though, Travis' brother helped Wednesday sit up with her back against the wall of the club. He was crouched down in front of her, inspecting her face.

"Baylor," Travis snarled. "Get that piece of trash out of here."

Baylor, whom I assumed was Travis' brother, seeing as they'd greeted each other as they had, followed his command. But only after he'd checked Wednesday over thoroughly, who was sitting down beside the building with her forehead resting on her upraised knees.

"Sure, bro."

Then he walked over to the man that Travis had taken down, grabbed him by the leather jacket, and then drug him over to the bike he'd been trying to get Wednesday to straddle in her inebriated state.

Once there, he threw him over the seat so his face was only inches away from the ground. Then he picked up a half-filled Dr. Pepper bottle—which might I add had dip spit in it—and poured it over the man's face.

I nearly vomited.

The liquid poured over the man's face, and started to go up his nose and into his partially open mouth.

Bile rose in my belly, and I had to turn away.

"Fuck." I covered my mouth with my hand. "That's the most disgusting thing I'd ever seen in my life."

I could handle a lot.

I was a nurse.

I'd seen babies being born. I'd worked a motorcycle wreck that had the man's face nearly ripped off. I'd even had to pack an ulcer wound that was all the way down to the bone on some man's ass.

None of that compared to thinking about some random person's spit cup full of tobacco juice going into another human being's mouth.

Not only was it unsanitary, but it was also disgusting and dangerous.

But, after witnessing him groping Wednesday while she was clearly under the influence, and trying to get her to stay on his bike while he did it…well, I didn't have much care or understanding for the man.

Travis' eyes caught mine, and he winked.

I lifted my lip in a silent snarl, causing him to laugh.

I then proceeded to flip him off, which only made him laugh harder.

"Get your girl home, Hannah," he ordered.

I looked at my 'girl,' who happened to now be lying on the dirty alley floor.

"Help me get her to my car?" I pleaded, holding my hands up in a praying motion.

He did it without me asking twice. Once Wednesday was in his arms—and I wouldn't be admitting that it caused me even the tiniest bit of jealousy—he took her to my car. A car I hadn't even told him was mine, and waited for me to open it for him.

Once he had her placed in my back seat, he closed the door, walked to me, placed a single kiss on my forehead, and was gone moments later.

His destination? The man that Baylor was talking to.

I chose to drive away instead of staying to watch what was about to happen to that man.

I could deny any knowledge of the incident…and that man would get what he deserved.

CHAPTER 4

Sometimes when I watch Travis make coffee and he smiles, I wonder who he just thought about pissing off today.
-Hannah's secret thoughts

Hannah

Present day

I juggled the car seat, as well as held Reggie's hand, as we crossed the parking lot and entered the store.

We were at the mall.

Reggie wanted something pretty to wear, and stupidly enough, I'd agreed to get it for her.

She was going to see her father this weekend, and she 'wanted to look pretty for her daddy.'

I knew that what she really wanted was to impress Joshua, but I didn't have the heart to tell her that Joshua wouldn't even notice. Joshua was too interested in his secretary, as well as his work, to care about his little girl.

The only thing that would make Joshua notice her would be if Reggie suddenly knew the secret to the stock exchange.

But even then, he'd only notice her long enough to get her secrets. Then he'd leave her on her own again, just like he did every time he deigned to see her.

Sure, Jefferson was only two hours from our hometown of Kilgore, Texas. But that didn't make much of a difference to Joshua. Anything over a twenty-minute drive was an inconvenience to him.

Which he let her know each and every time it was his turn to drive out here and get her for the weekend.

So there I was, with a two-month-old, and my eight-year-old, taking them to the mall on a Friday at four in the afternoon.

I'd forgotten TJ's stroller, and I had to either carry him in his car seat, or carry him in the infant carrier that he absolutely despised being in. There was something about how he was restrained that he didn't like, causing him to never quite settle down.

Which meant I was carrying my twelve-pound two-month-old, in his eight-pound car seat, juggling a diaper bag, as well as trying to hang onto Reggie who refused to cross the street still without holding my hand.

Not that that bothered me all that much. I loved holding Reggie's hand.

It'd been me and her for so very long, and she was growing up so godforsaken fast that I would take anything she was willing to give me.

It felt like just yesterday when she decided that she was going to walk instead of crawl. Run instead of walk. Talk instead of gesture. Ask to be put down instead of being held.

Hell, I couldn't remember the last time I'd helped give her a bath. It was like one day she decided that she no longer needed my assistance, and that was that.

"Ohhh!" she cried out the moment we crossed into the mall. "Can we get a cookie?"

I grinned.

I'd created a monster.

I loved Great American Cookie Factory. It was my guilty pleasure, and sure as shit, Reggie liked them, too.

My phone rang before we could so much as pass through the front doors, and I growled.

Before I could put down the infant carrier, though, it was taken out of my hands.

I gasped, my gaze snapping up as fear started to slice through me, and then closed my eyes in relief.

"You made it."

I'd called Travis about halfway to the mall and asked if he could come get TJ. It was the day before I would start working full-time, and not only did I need to run by the mall for Reggie, I also needed to run by the scrub store to get some different scrubs that would fit my more voluptuous hips.

When I was pregnant, I'd been wearing a few pairs that I'd bought from the Goodwill. There was no way in hell I was paying the exorbitant amount of money for new scrubs that would only fit for just a few short months. However, now that I was down to my regular size—almost—I decided that maybe I'd spring for some scrubs that were a little prettier, and not so worn out.

Hence the other reason I'd decided to agree to Reggie's pleading rather than tell her no like I'd wanted to.

"I did." Travis' deep voice had my heart fluttering.

Hell, anything the man did made my heart flutter.

We were right there, almost in this exact same spot, when I'd met him for the second time.

And the same thing happened then as it had today.

***

387 days ago

"You're the one who has holes in her scrubs," my new co-worker, Wednesday, commented dryly. "You asked where the best place to go was, and I, being the nice person that I am, volunteered to take you."

"I'll be there in a minute," I told her. "Okay?"

She rolled her eyes and started walking away, not bothering to look back.

I looked in disgust at the mall.

I hated shopping. I hated crowds, and most of all, I hated being in a mall that had me only inches away from the most fattening food in the city.

My eyes kept going back from the cookie display, to the way that Wednesday headed without me.

I was having a long, stern talk with myself about how much I did not need a cookie. But I couldn't help it.

They had my favorite. Double Doozies. With the chocolate icing instead of the white.

Oh, my God. They were so good.

And normally I could walk right past this display and not have a problem. Today, however, I was on my period. Today, I was feeling sorry for myself.

Today marked two entire days since I'd had one hell of a conversation with the hottest man alive.

I couldn't stop thinking about him.

Every time I turned around, my thoughts would stray to him. *What was he doing? Where was he at? Would I ever see him again?*

Annoyed with myself, I tried to take a step away but was held up by a male body sidling up beside me.

Which was the excuse I needed to stay.

Maybe just one tiny cookie. They made the ones they called the 'Mini Doozies.' Maybe just one…

"What are you getting?"

"I think one of the Doozies," I murmured, then stopped and turned when I realized that it wasn't the man behind the counter that had asked me that question, but the one standing beside me.

The moment that I saw his face, my breath stalled in my chest.

"I'm going to get a slice of the cake," he murmured, winking. "Are you getting the big one or the 'mini' one?" He paused. "I've had both. They don't taste the same. I think you should get the big one, and maybe just eat a quarter of it if you're planning on going with the mini."

I laughed.

"You think that if I have an entire giant-sized Double Doozie that I'll be able to eat 'just a quarter?'" I questioned him.

Was he crazy?

He shrugged. “You’re in incredible shape. Figure that you are able to control your appetite.”

I snorted. “Yeah, that’s a big fat no.”

He grunted.

“And it’s even worse when I’m on my period, like today,” I mentioned.

That was when I realized that I just told the man that was sexy as sin that I was on my period…*like he would want to know that.*

Oh, God.

If the ground could open up and swallow me whole, that’d be great.

“Good to know,” Travis said, not cracking a joke or even a smile. “My sister liked those.”

He pointed at the red velvet brownies, and I scrunched up my nose. “I’m not that fond of them myself.”

In fact, if there was one thing on this entire shelf display that I did not like, it was those.

When I was pregnant with Reggie, those had been the only thing that I could stomach for over a month, and throughout the rest of my pregnancy, I’d eaten them over and over and over again.

If I never saw another one of them again, it’d be too soon.

“Who’s next?”

I gestured for Travis to go—mostly because I wanted to check his ass out without him noticing—and he stepped forward. He said something quietly to the cashier who nodded, reached for two Double Doozies, took two slices of cookie cake, and then rang it all up.

When Travis turned around, my eyes snapped up to his and a guilty look crossed over my face at him catching me checking him out.

He didn't so much as tease me.

Instead, he handed over the Double Doozies he'd just ordered and walked away without saying a word, leaving me to watch.

"Man's hot."

I turned to the chick behind the counter and nodded.

"He is."

***

Present day

And he still was hot. Even a year later, he was hot as sin.

Sure, he was a little grayer around the temples, but a crazy ex-wife, a kid that hated you, and a newborn, would do that to a man.

Without even asking, he walked up to the cookie counter and ordered some cookies, even going as far as to have the worker make a Double Doozie with chocolate icing because he knew what I liked and they'd run out.

When he handed over my Doozie, as well as Reggie's, he winked. "Where to now?"

I licked my lips and looked away, my heart starting to ache.

God, I loved this man.

I loved him with my whole heart and soul, but I couldn't be with him.

It was the worst kind of situation anybody could ever be in.

And I couldn't even leave at this point because I had a kid with him, and I'd be no better than stupid Allegra if I did that to him.

So I stayed, despite my heart hurting each and every time I saw him.

"Crazy 8, I guess," I croaked. "If she doesn't find anything there, we'll go to Kohl's."

And that's what we did.

To all passersby, we were like one nice, big, happy family.

Only, they'd be wrong.

CHAPTER 5

I'm confident my last words will be, "Are you fucking kidding me?"
-Travis' secret thoughts

Travis

370 days ago

It was the first time I'd seen her with her kid.

It was the first time she'd seen me with mine.

"You look a little lost," she said to me.

I gave her a dry look.

"What gave that away?" I teased.

She looked at me, surrounded by all the other moms at their Mommy & Me Tea Party at the school, and grinned.

"I think it was the fact that you're the only man in a roomful of moms," she countered back.

I winked at her and turned back to my tea.

I didn't like tea. Well, let me rephrase that. I liked tea. What I did not like was tea that was not sweet. This green tea, or Earl Grey, or whatever the fuck it was, tasted like mold.

What I wouldn't do for a huge glass of McDonald's sweet tea right now to wash this disgusting taste out of my mouth. Or a beer, but I highly doubted that the school would approve of me bringing a cooler full of ice cold beer to their stupid Mommy & Me Tea bullshit.

However, there was not a single thing in the world that I wouldn't do for my little girl, and if I had to sit at a Mommy & Me Tea brunch date with her at her school to make her smile, then I'd fucking do it. Twice, if I had to.

It had never occurred to me that she would be there, though.

She didn't look like she'd had a kid, let alone did she look old enough to have one that was the same age as mine!

But it was what it was, and now I had something pretty to stare at beside my kid who was clearly not too happy being where she was at, and with who she was with.

She wanted her mother here.

I'd wanted her mother here.

Allegra, however, had something pressing to do, and decided to do that instead of this.

Knowing what this meant to my kid, I'd decided to bite the bullet and come. Unfortunately, I was straight off of a job, and I was covered in grease. It was ground into my pants, covered my shirt, and I was fairly sure that I had it in my hair.

Alex, being the phobic girl that she was, refused to even give me a hug.

A trait that came from her fucking mother. Her fucking mother who refused to do the exact same thing when I was dirty like I was, too.

Was it too hard to ask for a fuckin' hug after a long day at work? Was it too much to ask for a woman to not care if her clothes got dirty?

Because that's what I wanted. A woman that was going to love me unconditionally—dirt and all.

But Allegra had shown her true colors over and over again, and I fucking hated…

"You want some of mine?"

I looked over to find her pulling a chair out, sitting at the tiny mini-human desk right beside me.

She looked funny with her knees up by her chest, and I was sure that I looked just as silly—if not sillier.

"Yours what?" I questioned, looking at her.

"My tea." She shook the glass.

I stared at the McDonald's cup in reverence.

"What do you have?" I questioned.

She rolled her eyes and held out the glass. "Sweet tea."

"You read my mind," I told her but didn't reach to take the glass. "But no, I'm not going to take your glass."

She shook the cup, and the ice and tea inside of the cup swished. "Come on. I'm not going to drink any more. I've already had three of them when I had lunch with Wednesday."

"Who is Wednesday?" Alex asked, a slight sneer in her voice. "What kind of name is Wednesday, anyway?"

Hannah's eyes turned from me to my kid's, and she grinned, smiling so beautifully that my heart actually squeezed.

"Have you ever seen the Addams Family?" she questioned. "There's a girl that's around your age in it. Her name was Wednesday."

Alex didn't crack a smile or even act like she was interested in anything that Hannah had to say.

In fact, the moment that Hannah started to talk, she turned her head away and looked at the women across the room from us.

I didn't need to look at those women. They were friends of Allegra's and had already expressed their distaste with having me here instead of Allegra—luckily not in front of my child, at least.

"Are you going to drink that, Mister?"

I looked over to see Hannah's child staring at me expectantly.

I grinned and pushed my cup and saucer in her direction. "Have at it, pretty girl."

That term of endearment had Alex's head whipping around like I'd said something naughty, and I guess that in Alex terms, I might have.

Sweet Girl had been her nickname, along with many others that I'd termed her over the years since she'd been alive.

I hadn't called her 'Sweet Girl' in a long time, and likely she realized that.

If I was being honest, Alex hadn't been 'sweet' for a while.

Her mother had ruined her. Treated her like she was some higher person in society and like her shit didn't stink.

Allegra and I had split a while ago—years if we were counting the amount of time in which we'd been together but not 'together,' at least in the biblical sense.

Since we'd separated, and later divorced, Allegra had made it a point to mold my daughter into the little asshole she'd turned into. It sucked. I missed my little girl.

This staring, glaring, name calling kid wasn't the one that I knew and loved.

Sure, I still loved Alex, no matter what. But this kid wasn't the one that had begged me to take her fishing. Wasn't the one that had pleaded with me to ride in my 'toe tuck.'

She was Allegra's child. She was everything that I hated in Allegra.

"Thank you!" Hannah's girl smiled, her flashy white teeth revealing one single tooth missing.

Which reminded me.

"Oh, hey, baby," I turned to Alex. "Did the Tooth Fairy bring you some money for your lost tooth?"

I'd gotten a text from Allegra that Alex had lost her first tooth about a week ago. Yes, you heard that right. A week ago.

"The Tooth Fairy isn't real, Dad." Alex's snide comment had me clenching my fists. "You know how Mommy doesn't like to lie to me."

Unlike you was left unsaid.

Excuse the fuck out of me if I wanted my kid to believe in the unreal for just a little bit longer. *Excuse-fucking-me!*

"What?" Hannah's little girl asked in dejected surprise. "Mama?"

I winced, forgetting for a moment that we weren't alone.

I looked over to Hannah apologetically.

"I'm sorry," I told her. "We're just gonna go sit over there."

I got up and gave Alex a glare that clearly meant ‘move your ass or I’ll beat it.’

She moved.

I sat down on the next stupid white chair and turned my angry eyes to Alex.

“You know,” I told her, “that was a jerk move.”

Alex batted her eyelashes. “I don’t like her.”

I gritted my teeth.

“Who?”

“Either.”

“Why?” I questioned. “What did they ever do to you?”

Alex crossed her arms over her chest, and the move let her shirt that was already too low for my taste to begin with fall down even lower.

I held my tongue. Barely.

“Why are you even here?” she countered, refusing to answer my question.

“I’m here because I know that this meant so much to you,” I told her honestly. “And I know that you said something about wanting to go.”

She looked down at her lap, a trace of discomfort gracing her face before it fled altogether.

I could see the moment that she decided to be ugly instead of apologizing.

“Well, I don’t want you here.”

Two hours later, I was thankful that I had the choice of whether to take Alex home or not.

Thankfully, her mother would be here to pick her up from the Mommy and Me class, because I was so ready to go it wasn't even funny.

My daughter was acting like a royal asshole, and I didn't want to be around her any longer.

Sure, after I calmed down, I would be back to loving my kid no matter what, but right now, with her anger and rude words that she'd tossed at me over the last two hours, I was ready for it to be over.

I looked down and away from Allegra's car, knowing from experience if I let her see me and stopped, I would be forced to talk to her.

I thought I'd gotten away with it, too. But then I heard my name.

I hesitated, but it was enough for Allegra to notice me. Then call out to me.

"You're being paged," Hannah whispered.

I felt Hannah's hand on my bicep, and turned, pausing in my death march.

"I hear," I muttered darkly. "I'm heading over now."

She patted my arm and started to go, but I stopped her by reaching for her retreating hand.

"I'm sorry again for what Alex said," I told her. "She's been so rude lately, to everyone including me. But I never in a million years would've thought she'd reveal something like that."

She smiled and reached up to pull a white string off the side of my shirt before replying.

"It'll be okay. Reggie's a tough girl. Reggie and I come from tough stock."

I sighed. “Just wish you didn’t have to. She disappointed me today, and I’ll have a talk with her mother to be sure that that doesn’t happen again.”

“I know you heard me, asshole!”

I gritted my teeth and turned.

Only I made a mistake. I allowed Hannah to witness Allegra’s venom.

And in doing so, I familiarized the two women with one another, even if they weren’t formally ‘introduced.’

“I heard you, Allegra,” I told her bluntly, making my words steely and hard. “But I’m apologizing to another parent for your daughter’s rudeness. Please, give me a moment.”

Allegra’s eyes narrowed.

Wrong thing to say, apparently.

“You shouldn’t have to apologize for anything she did. Our child is perfect.”

I wanted to laugh at that.

Our child was anything but perfect. She was exactly like Allegra, and that sucked.

“Actually, there was something to apologize for. Excuse me for another minute.”

I turned my back on Allegra, which pissed her off even more.

And that was when I made my mistake.

I completely missed the anger on Allegra’s face, but I would be feeling it, even months later.

***

Present day

"Well, I don't want you here."

Where had I heard those words before?

My memories drifted away from that god-awful day.

That was the day that Allegra had found out about Hannah, and the last time that I ever *willingly* said anything to Allegra about Hannah.

The bitch was always in my face, and the moment she heard about Hannah and me, it was like the gloves had come off.

It would take me a while to see what Allegra was doing, but eventually, I'd caught on.

And now, I hated her even more.

"What do you mean your hours were changed?"

Hannah looked away.

"I got back to work, but since I wasn't there the last six weeks, they decided that they wanted to change up the hours. I'm only working half the day now."

Hannah's words, although soft and unconcerned, were something concerning to me.

"Apply at the hospital in…"

Hannah was already shaking her head.

"I can't," she said. "That's too far. I don't want to work twelve hours, at least not yet. I can make it."

I knew she could make it. I would make sure she could make it. But to do that, she'd have to give Reggie less…or likely herself since she wouldn't allow Reggie to suffer.

I wouldn't allow that.

"Did they tell you why the changes?" I inquired.

She looked away.

"Hannah?"

She shrugged.

"Hannah," I snapped. "What is it?"

Hannah opened her mouth to say something, but then a patient pushed through the door.

Hannah waved me off and went to the man who was clearly struggling to breathe, and I was left with TJ in my arms, wondering what in the hell had happened.

It didn't take me long.

As soon as Hannah left, the receptionist, Daneen, sidled up.

She was a middle-aged woman with graying brown hair, a quick smile, and a love for Hannah that made me happy that she had someone in her corner like that.

But with that came the fierce protectiveness.

"It was the woman with the black dress."

My brows went up.

"What woman?"

Daneen looked at where Hannah had disappeared, and then back to me.

"A woman came in two days ago. She expressed her willingness to donate to the clinic. I only heard a little bit before the doctor disappeared with her into his office, but it was enough for me to hear that 'some changes would have to be made' before she invested."

CHAPTER 6

Napping together is my kind of date.
-Hannah's secret thoughts

Hannah

Present day

The turning point in mine and Travis' relationship was the day that his sister was in the accident that killed her brother's wife and children.

It was hard to believe that it'd already been a year.

In all honesty, I was glad that it passed as fast as it did.

They say that time healed all wounds. And my hope that was one day, time would heal Dante's wounds.

Seeing him that day, so broken and so obviously hurting, had been something that made me realize two things.

One, that life was not guaranteed. Two, that I needed to get my head out of my ass when it came to Travis. If I wanted him, I needed to do something about it. I needed to cross that line I'd drawn in the sand.

The one that he'd been toeing since the moment I put it there.

What had started the beginning of the end for us was me hearing about the tragedy.

***

366 days ago

"Did you see that the firefighters blocked off the entrance to the street?"

I nodded. "Yeah, what happened?"

Wednesday looked like she was going to be sick.

"There was a wreck. A woman was in an accident. She ended up killing every single person in the car but herself."

My belly tightened. "Oh, no. What happened?"

She shook her head. "I don't know, to be honest. What I was able to find out came from Gallagher. He was behind the woman before she wrecked. Since he was so close to work, they let him through instead of holding him at the scene since they blocked off two blocks. They think the woman was under the influence of either drugs or alcohol. She was life-flighted out of here."

"How many people were in the car?"

While we spoke, I pulled the med cart over and started to count the pills, double-checking that number with the number we had in the system.

The system that Hostel's small clinic had was outdated at best and desperately needed to be updated. However, with little to no funds, it was very hard to accomplish much of anything. We were lucky that the government paid us what they did at this point.

I'd never set out to come to a place like this. I loved my job at the hospital in Kilgore. What I didn't like, however, was being so near to my ex—which prompted the move in the first place.

"Two kids, two adults," Wednesday answered. "The kids and the mother died. The driver is fine."

A sense of foreboding went through me.

All accidents, small and big, were terrible. Losing anyone in an accident sucked. What was worse, though, than losing a life? Losing a child whose life had barely started.

Hell, it could've had a mass casualty, and as long as the people's lives that were lost weren't children, it would be okay. Not right off the bat, but it would be okay.

Losing a child, though? The memories of those deaths had a way of staying with you for a long time, lingering, waiting to pounce when you least expected them to.

"Did they release the names?"

Wednesday shook her head. "There was no reason to. Everyone knew who it was. The father lost it in the middle of the freakin' road earlier. Took three of his brothers to hold him back from going to help."

I closed my eyes and looked down at my feet.

I knew who it was.

There was only one family in the entire town that everyone knew…that everyone would talk about.

"It's the Hails?"

She nodded. "Yeah. I heard that they're having to put Dante in a cell at the police station to keep him under control."

I wouldn't doubt it.

I'd have lost it too had my children been killed…by my own sister at that.

"I gotta go." I looked around. "I'll be right back."

I didn't know what I was going to do, but something told me that I needed to find Travis and make sure that he was okay.

Leaving the clinic with only one thing on my mind, I forwent getting into my truck, and instead decided to hurry down the sidewalk to Hail Auto Recovery—which was about two blocks away.

Since our town was set up for downtown traffic, I had no problem getting there, even though I hadn't been there before.

Since I'd met Travis, I'd asked around about him.

I'd found out that the towing company was directly next to the club that I'd met him in—which Travis and his brother also owned—though he'd never said.

Sure enough, two blocks later, I was in front of the towing company.

There were trucks parked every which way all over the huge parking lot. Men were standing around, talking in close-knit circles.

There were a few women as well, but I bypassed them all in search of someone I knew.

I didn't know what I was doing, but something inside my heart was telling me that I needed to be here.

That I needed to offer Travis the chance to talk if he needed it.

So, I did.

I walked straight through all the trucks and milling people, cut straight into what looked like an office, and immediately came to a stop.

The minute I was inside, I could hear the yelling.

"Let me out of here!"

My eyes widened.

“I’m not letting you out.”

That was Travis. His voice was calm, but he looked anything but calm.

He had his head pressed against a clearly broken wooden door, his hand splayed on the cool wood like he was offering the man behind it support through sheer force of will.

He was in coveralls that were tied around the waist, and the knees had stains that looked suspiciously like something brown and gooey.

“Let me out.”

Those three words, coming from a clearly broken adult man, were enough to send heartache through me. It was like someone had coated those words with steel, and shoved them straight through my heart.

I could literally feel my heart breaking for the poor man.

“Trav.”

The first tear left my eye.

“Please, Trav. I need to see them.”

“I don’t have that authority,” Travis choked. “If I did, I would let you out of there right now. I’d take you to the hospital, and I’d give you that, but I don’t have the authority. They already told me on the phone that they wouldn’t let you back.”

“I do.”

Travis’ face turned from the door toward me.

“Please, Trav.”

The man’s devastated voice continued, unable to hear my words.

Travis, though…well, he heard. He was looking at me with such an intense light that I nearly took a step back.

"You do?"

I nodded, then paused. "They're at the morgue?"

Travis' eyes were so intense that I had to take a deep breath.

He nodded.

"I have access to it. Let me make a few calls."

And that was how, twenty minutes later, I led two very distraught men into the morgue.

"Don't touch anything, y'all," I whispered to the two men.

Dead eyes locked on mine.

He didn't have to tell me what he thought of my words. I could read every single emotion that was filing through his brain.

Rage. Devastation. Anger. Hurt.

He was literally broken and looked nothing like the man I'd heard about from the townspeople.

We walked into the morgue, and I gave Dave, the night security officer that I'd helped at the clinic with a very personal problem a few weeks ago, a nod. He waved me through, and I stopped just inside the door.

"They're in lockers four, five, and six," I told them. "Remember, don't touch."

Travis walked forward, stopped in front of locker six, and pulled it open.

The sound that left his throat at seeing the tiny child, blue and so still, was a sound that would forever stay with me as long as I lived.

But the sound from the man who was frozen at my side?

I didn't breathe for an entire minute.

And I only took a breath when the sound quit, and Dante fell to his knees.

CHAPTER 7

Am I the only one running out of people I like?
-Coffee Cup

Travis

349 days ago

I walked up to the convenience store, my goal being a Gatorade and a bag of pork wheels, and almost missed the woman that was headed in at an angle right along with me.

She had her face steady on her phone, so I noticed her before she noticed me.

Grinning, I opened the door and held it open, all the while she kept her eyes downcast on her phone.

"Thank you," she muttered distractedly.

"You're welcome."

At the sound of my voice, her head snapped up so fast that she started to bobble her phone.

I caught it before it could hit the ground, and instead of handing it to her, slipped it into the back pocket of her jeans.

"T-thank you," she murmured. "How are you?"

Her voice was low, intimate.

"I'm getting there, honey," I told her, thankful that she asked. "Where ya headed?"

She smiled weakly.

"I'm in desperate need of a Butterfinger."

I grinned at the thought of her being in desperate need of a candy bar. "Pork wheels and a Gatorade for me."

She giggled. "What a balanced lunch we're having."

Wasn't that right?

Hostel didn't have much in the way of restaurants. One awesome burger place that I'd never have time to get to with the hour that I had left of my lunch break. A small taco stand that was always busy—lunch or not. And then the gas station.

I chose the gas station, but instead of getting my taquitos—fried corn tortillas filled with cheesy goodness—I decided that I was going with something different. And less heartburn-inducing.

"Yeah, a balanced lunch." I chuckled. "That's exactly what it is."

She laughed all the way to the candy aisle.

I bypassed that aisle for the drink aisle and then grabbed the pork wheels on the way to the checker who was standing there looking bored.

"That all?" he asked me.

I pointed to the Butterfinger in Hannah's hands. "That too."

"You don't…"

I looked at her over my shoulder. "You don't pay when I'm around, sweet cheeks."

She blinked. "You did not just call me sweet cheeks."

I shrugged. "Would you rather honey bun?"

She huffed out a breath of air. "I'd rather my name."

I winked at her and offered the man a twenty, then collected my change before holding the door for Hannah to walk out in front of me.

She did, and I got to admire her fine ass in her jeans.

She surprised me when she turned around, though.

"You want to grab something to eat later?"

I opened my mouth to reply, but she beat me to it.

"I'll be at the burger joint in town. They're having a PTA meeting there, and I don't want to be alone."

I snorted. "What makes you think I want to go to a PTA meeting?"

She shrugged. "I don't know. We can act like we're there to be there, but really just ignore them and do our own thing."

I thought about it for all of two seconds.

I really liked this one, and she was nice to my smart-mouthed daughter even when she didn't deserve it.

"I think that sounds like a fuckin' plan."

Before I could say anything more, I got a text message.

"Shit, hold on," I said when I saw Hannah about to reply.

I pulled out my phone and glanced at the screen, my brows furrowing.

"Sorry, it's my daughter's teacher asking for me to come up there." I dropped the phone back into my pocket. "I'll be there."

Her smile was brilliant.

"I'll be waiting…with bells on."

The smile that lit my face at that, and all the way to the school, would've thrown red flags among not just one, but all of my brothers.

That smile died the minute I got into the school and heard what Alex's teacher had to say.

I stared at my daughter's teacher with dawning horror.

"She what?"

"She has lice."

My mouth dropped open.

"She washes herself relentlessly!" I groaned.

My kid hated dirt. And when I say hate, I meant *hate*. She despised it. Loathed it. Anything that came as possibly 'dirty' to her, she wouldn't go near it.

The teacher, Ms. Captain, smiled sadly.

"That's sometimes the contributing factor in lice cases, Mr. Hail," she apologized. "Lice likes clean homes, and little kids that have clean hair offer the most hospitable environment."

I nodded in stunned horror.

Oh, God. *Lice?*

What the fuck did I do with that?

"I'll take her home to her mother…"

The teacher was already shaking her head. "I've told Ms. Hail. She refused to come get her. I know that technically we can't send her home due to discrimination laws, but she's miserable. She's itching, and it's disrupting her schoolwork. I didn't know what else to do."

I nodded.

Why didn't it surprise me that Allegra refused to help her own daughter?

"Okay." I looked at my watch. I wouldn't be making my date with Hannah. "I'll take her home now. Thank you for calling me. I don't want her miserable."

She smiled sadly at me.

"She can return to school tomorrow…"

I held up my hand. "I'll keep her home for the rest of the week."

She looked relieved.

"Thank you."

It was said so quietly that I had to strain to hear it.

My daughter and I walked out of the school minutes later, and I felt like my skin was crawling.

My first step the moment I got into the truck was to Google 'head lice,' and what I found literally made my breath catch.

Goddammit, lice were creepy.

Now my head itched.

But instead of freaking way the fuck out, I drove to the pharmacy, bought every box of Rid they had, and drove home.

The next step was to quarantine her to the kitchen. All of my furniture was cloth, and what I read in the articles said that you should clean everything cloth.

Since my daughter hadn't been here in two weeks, I felt it was safe enough to say that I didn't have an infestation in my house.

Her head, after closer examination, did.

I wanted to vomit.

I was a man. I could deal with a good deal of shit.

Hell, I was a Marine for twelve years. I'd seen blood, death, gore. You name it, I saw it.

I could deal with roaches and all kinds of gross shit—you see a lot when you're repossessing cars—and not miss a wink of sleep.

But bugs crawling in my daughter's hair? Apparently, that was the icky point.

My phone pinged as I saturated my daughter's head with the first bottle of shampoo.

I ignored it, soaking my daughter's beautiful hair in it until every inch of it wasn't shining with the oily goo. Then I washed my hands and said, "Now don't move for another ten minutes, okay?"

My daughter sneered at me.

What she didn't do was move.

Whatever.

After making sure my hands were clean of the oily mess, I picked up my phone and read the first text message.

Unknown (12:33 pm.): **Don't forget to bring your cash. They're selling booster tickets.**

I smiled for the first time since I left her.

Travis (12:43 pm): **Change of plans. My daughter has head lice. Everything itches (on me, not on her.)**

I programmed her phone number into my phone and glanced up at my daughter.

"You okay?"

"Wonderful," she shot back.

Great!

Not.

"You want some chocolate milk?" I asked her, starting to head to the cabinet to get her a cup.

"No thanks," she said, stunning me with her answer. "It's fattening."

My mouth dropped open.

"Who told you that?"

"Mom."

Fucking Allegra.

My phone pinged, so I shut the cabinet door and went for it.

Hannah (12:45 pm): **Oh, no! Do you need any help?**

I grunted, liking that she was willing to help.

What I didn't want was for her to have the chance of getting it, so I said no.

An hour later, I was still trying to pick the little bitches out of her hair, and I knew that this wasn't going to be done on my own. So I bit the bullet and sent the text that I didn't want to send.

Travis (1:45 pm): **I can't get them out. Who the hell invented this stupid goddamn metal brush? It's not picking up anything!**

Hannah (1:47 pm): **I'll be there in ten minutes. Give me directions.**

I did, and hit send, thankful that someone was coming to help me.

I could've called my mother, and probably should have, but the idea of having Hannah here while I went through this was enough to make me ignore the idea of doing the right thing.

I'd just gotten through another miniscule amount of hair when I heard the doorbell ring.

My heart leapt.

"Be right back, honey," I said.

When I opened the door, it was to find Hannah standing there, a large bag in her hands, and in a new t-shirt and a pair of shorts.

"I brought sustenance. Take me to your leader."

I snorted and opened it wide.

"Thank you, Hannah."

She winked. "No problem."

And she proved that by spending the next three hours picking the world's worst thing ever out of my kid's hair.

***

Present day

"I don't understand," I groaned to the sky. "Why is it always her making waves?"

"I've told you once, I've told you a million times," Reed grunted as he watched the TV in my living room. "You're fucking her over. You're fucking everybody over for that bitch's promise that she won't do anything, yet, she *is* doing stuff. Your kid is a fucking asshole. I'm sorry to say that bro, but she's Allegra's mini-me, and she's damn mean. She won't even look at me without sneering. I didn't even *do* anything to her."

That was true, and the urge to jump to my child's defense was high.

Yet, I couldn't argue with him.

He was right.

Hannah, Reggie, and I had done our part in this. We'd done everything right. We'd bowed to everything that Allegra requested, yet Allegra continued to fuck me over. And in turn, continued to turn our child against me.

It hurt.

And obviously, I wasn't the only one affected.

My mom was devastated. Allegra literally hated her guts, and after losing one granddaughter who moved out of state, and the other two grandchildren in the car crash…well, that was just the icing on the shit cake.

I looked around the empty house.

TJ was at daycare, Reggie was at school, and Hannah was at work.

This was my first day off in weeks, and I didn't know what to do with myself.

I'd been on my way into work when my brother had called, telling me in no uncertain terms that I needed to turn my life around.

"What brought this visit on?" I asked, taking a sip of my beer.

It was ten o'clock in the morning, but I needed it.

I literally thought I might die without the beer.

"I saw Hannah's brother today."

My stomach clenched.

"Where?"

"The hotel."

Fuck!

"What's he doing here?"

I didn't bother to ask him why he was at the hotel. I knew why.

"He's here to see the kids. Hasn't seen them in a while."

I pursed my lips. "Did he bring Nikki and the kids?"

He nodded.

Wonderful.

I'd have to depart my residence to allow them the ability to come over and visit without adding that certain level of uneasiness that was always around when Michael and I were in the same room.

Not that I could blame him for hating me.

If anyone had done what I'd done to Hannah to my sister, I'd feel the same freakin' way.

Goddammit.

Two hours later, I left my house for my brother's house, and stayed there while Hannah, Reggie, and TJ caught up with their Uncle Michael. I'd return once Michael and his crew left for the hotel they would be staying at during their visit.

Lucky for me, I didn't have to sleep on my brother's couch because he'd rented a room. Unlucky for me, Michael was just leaving as I was arriving. I was treated to a glare from Michael, and a sad, uncomfortable grin from Hannah.

Just wonderful.

CHAPTER 8

Apparently, rock bottom has a basement. Who knew?
-Hannah's secret thoughts

Hannah

"Mom!" Reggie pulled on my hand. "Look at the dog that Travis has! It looks just like Mogley!"

Mogley used to be my ex-husband's hunting dog. Right around the time we got divorced, Mogley started to go downhill. With no more use for his hunting dog now that Mogley was too old to hunt, he had no use for the dog.

When I'd heard that he was about to take him to a shelter, I'd taken Mogley with me.

Mogley had lived out the rest of his days in comfort, and he'd passed about ten months ago during the night.

That was the night that I'd called Travis in tears, unsure what I should do with him.

***

347 days ago

I walked out into the hall, discomforted when I'd realized that Mogley hadn't followed into my room after an hour or so.

And I knew, the moment that I saw the large black lump on the floor, that it was Mogley.

What I hadn't thought, was that he wouldn't be breathing.

Sure, he was nearly eleven years old, but the ol' boy had a lot of heart left in him.

I'd thought I had another few years with him at least.

I didn't think, not in a million years, that he would die.

"Moge?" I called.

The black form didn't move, and my brows furrowed.

"Moge, it's bedtime!" I called to him, clapping my hands. "Come on, let's go!"

Mogley still didn't move.

Worried now, I flipped on the light, and my heart dropped.

"Moge?"

Mogley was facing me, his unseeing eyes staring toward my door.

"Moge?" My voice broke.

This time there were tears in my eyes.

"No," I croaked. "Please no."

Reggie would break. She'd literally break when she heard the news.

So, in order not to wake her, I let my tears fall silently.

"Oh, baby." I dropped down to my knees, running my fingers down my baby's soft fur. "I'm going to miss you like crazy."

I ran my hand down the length of his body, then back up again. He'd been so big…so full of life. It didn't feel right that he wasn't attacking me with his tongue like he normally would have.

He was lying so still.

A tear fell to my bare thigh.

Sniffling, I stood up and walked to my room, slipping on my shorts and tennis shoes.

My intention was to lift him, to bring him outside…to do what, I didn't know. But I knew I couldn't leave him there. The moment that Reggie got up, she'd see him.

She'd know instantly.

Which meant I had to do this now, in the middle of the night.

Except I found out really quick that the dead weight of a one-hundred-pound dog was a lot different than one hundred pounds of moving dog.

I got him a whole foot from where he was lying before I realized that I wouldn't be able to do it myself.

"Shit," I wiped away more tears. "Shit, shit, shit, shit."

I scanned through my memory, wondering who I should call. Each time I'd think of someone, I'd quickly dismiss them.

I had neighbors, but not any that I would trust coming in my house.

I also had Wednesday, but since I wasn't sure she could help me move him anymore than I could, I knew that there was only one person that I could call.

And the moment that he answered, I knew that he'd come.

"Everything okay?"

"I need your help."

He didn't even hesitate.

He came, helped me bury my friend, and then held me until Reggie woke up early.

Then, when my daughter found out about Mogley, he held her, too.

It was the single best day, and worst day, of my life.

Four hours later, my brother had my daughter, and I was at the front door to Travis' place.

I'd buried my canine friend today with a man that I felt had my back just as much as I'd had his.

We'd become friends over the last couple weeks. We'd seen each other on and off, but each time we came into contact, sparks would fly.

I knew I wasn't the only one feeling them. I knew it. I felt it in my very core.

So that was what had me standing on the porch of a man that'd done nothing more than offer me a shoulder to cry on, and save me from myself, each time we'd spent any length of time together.

I knocked on the door and felt my heart lurch when he opened it.

"Hannah?"

There was no hesitation inside of me at all.

I moved.

Pushing him with my hands on his chest, I went up onto my tippy toes and laid my mouth straight on his.

"I need you," I said the moment I pulled my lips from his.

It'd been a short, sweet kiss.

But, by the look on Travis' face, it'd gotten the point across.

Before I could do so much as explain myself, he was on me.

I had my back against his closed front door, and my legs around his hips, gasping as his mouth slammed down onto mine.

He was like a wild beast.

His beard was rasping against the sensitive skin of my neck, and his eyes were boring straight into mine.

At the same time, his hands were slipping under my shirt, and then shoving it up and over my head moments later. The next thing that went was my bra, which he deftly unclipped and let fall to the floor the moment I got my arms out of it.

He stopped at my mouth, only to drop that talented tongue to the tip of my nipple, lathing and sucking it as he practically worshipped me.

"Trav," I moaned, fisting my hands in his hair.

He growled something unintelligible, and then switched to the other nipple.

My hands trailed down his back, relishing in the play of muscles that rippled over his strong shoulders as he hoisted me up higher on his hips.

And his reason why was answered moments later when I heard the distinct clink-clink of his belt buckle being undone.

I bit my lip and studied him, running my hands down his side.

"I'm a fucking wreck," he told me. "I have a brother that is one crayon short of fucked up. My ex-wife is a bitch who's turning my kid into someone that nobody likes, and I'm a workaholic."

I blinked and stared.

"So?"

He didn't crack a smile. "Well, I'm so fucking lost that I don't know where to start to find my way again. If there was any sense of honor inside me at all, I'd tell you this was a bad fucking idea."

I stared at him for a few long moments. "I have an ex-husband that calls every three weeks to make sure that I got my payment. My daughter waits for him at our door every Wednesday and Friday night hoping that this will be the week that he comes. That dog you buried? He gave it to me because he didn't want it anymore. His new woman is allergic to dogs. Oh, and let's not forget that I've not had sex in well over five years, three of those I was married. I have a job that I'm not too sure I want to keep, and an overprotective brother who comes down once a week. I'll raise you ten."

He grunted in reply.

Then, without another word, he hooked two arms around my ass and carried me to his bedroom.

"Well, as long as we're agreeing that this is a bad idea," he dropped me. "Let's get started."

***

Present day

"What's with the dog?" I asked cautiously.

"It's a bribe," he told me. "My daughter said she'd only love me again if I bought her a puppy."

My mouth fell open in shock.

"She did not."

He smiled, but it didn't reach his eyes.

"She did."

My stomach tightened. "You know, right, that she was just saying that. She knows how allergic you are to them."

I remembered him picking Mogley up, and immediately breaking out in hives wherever Mogley's fur touched him.

It'd been horrible.

By the time Travis was done, he'd broken out in hives from wrist all the way up to his neck.

He'd told me that it was only a temporary thing, but I saw the discomfort in his eyes as he'd left that night.

And when I'd visited him a few hours later, he'd still had those hives.

He hadn't acted like it bothered him at all, but still.

"She knows that I'm allergic."

My mouth pinched shut. "She wouldn't have made that request of you. It has to be Allegra trying to be funny."

Travis shrugged. "You like dogs. Reggie is always asking for more. As long as you take care of him, and do all the loving that he's going to need, then I don't think it'll matter, will it?"

Technically, that was true. Travis could be around the dog, as long as he didn't touch the dog. The dog would have to stay off the furniture, or at least the furniture that Travis sat on. I'd have to make sure that I washed his clothes and put them away the instant that they were hung up instead of leaving them on the couch for a few days. Because it was inevitable that dog hair would get everywhere if I did.

I licked my lips, knowing that he wouldn't budge on this.

So, instead, I walked over to where Reggie was cuddling the dog and scratched the cute little puppy's fluffy head.

"Yeah, Trav. I'll help."

My brother glared at Travis, making me breathe out in frustration.

Michael and Travis likely would never get along. Even when Travis did something nice like buy my daughter a puppy that he knew would cause him discomfort.

CHAPTER 9

"As fuck" is my favorite unit of measurement.
-Fact of Life

Travis

Present day

"It's all right, Tobias," I said into the phone. "I'm calling him next."

"Let me know if you get a hold of him," Tobias sighed. "Oh, and I forgot to ask. How is the dog doing?"

Tobias had been the one to find me the chocolate lab puppy. He'd even gone as far as to meet me halfway with the dog.

I'd only broken out in hives for about thirty minutes before my Benadryl had kicked in, and since then, I'd taken a constant dose of the stuff.

My throat hadn't stopped itching since I'd gotten the dog.

As for Dante? Well, I already knew what he'd do.

I didn't reply at first, contemplating what to say.

We both knew that the possibility was low that he'd answer, but we'd try.

"The dog's good, Toab-Toab. Hannah's doing a superb job cleaning up the mess I left in her lap."

At my words, Tobias started to laugh. "Have a good one, bro."

Tobias said goodbye, and I immediately went back to my phone app and dialed Dante's number.

He, unsurprisingly, didn't answer.

"Dante," I said into my phone, pinching the bridge of my nose. "Please call me. Call any of us. We just want to know that you're okay."

I hadn't seen my brother in well over a month and a half. He'd completely gone off the grid since I'd seen him last, and it was an odd feeling.

Dante was normally the man that all of us could depend on. When he was the one hit with the tragedy, none of us knew what to do. How to react.

And honestly, he didn't either.

I secretly thought that was why he'd stayed away as he had, because he wasn't handling it all that well. *Though, who the fuck could blame him?*

Someone knocked on my office door, and I put the phone down with a soft thump.

After rubbing my face with my hands roughly, I said, "Come in."

Today was the anniversary of my sister's suicide. The day that my sister had decided that taking her own life was the answer to the problems that she faced.

Not that my sister didn't have her problems. They would've broken anybody.

When my sister was a teenager, Tobias' good friend had raped her. Repeatedly.

She'd never fully recovered. Then, she'd gotten into drugs—which she'd been on the night that she'd been driving Dante's family home.

After that day, she'd sobered up…or at least we'd thought that she had.

Which had been all of our faults. Tobias had really been the only one to stay on her hard. The rest of us had just been tired of it…which had been our own selfish protection act. We didn't want to deal with it anymore. We were all sad, worn down, and had our own problems.

And honestly, we thought she was handling it better than she had been. It'd been our fatal mistake.

My hands were still on my face, my fingers pressing into both eyes. Which meant that I didn't see her walk in.

Not until she touched my face.

"You okay?"

I dropped my hands and looked at the love of my life. The woman that I wanted, and couldn't have.

But then a thought occurred to me.

Dante had had it all.

He'd had a wife. Two children that he adored with all of his heart. A great business.

He'd had everything that he could've ever asked for…and then he'd lost it.

He'd lost it, and maybe would never find something like that ever again.

Me? I'd never been happy.

Sure, I had a child. Yes, I loved her with all of my heart.

But her mother was poisoning her. Allegra was shaping her into a person that I knew wouldn't lead to good things if we weren't careful.

I'd let Allegra control my life. I'd made a mistake when I married her. When I'd entrusted her with my hopes and dreams.

Now, Allegra challenged those dreams…threatened to ruin them.

And I was letting her.

I'd told Alex about the dog, excited to see her excited for once, and she'd sneered.

She'd sneered.

That was when I knew I wouldn't win.

"Are you okay?"

I closed my eyes, and then swiveled in my chair and buried my face into her stomach, while threading my arms around her body. My arms wrapped around her thighs, pulling her in tight.

Her belly was soft, and she smelled so fucking good.

"I'm not okay," I told her, pushing my face further into her soft belly. "I'm so far from okay that I don't think I'll ever be okay again."

She was hesitant to touch me.

I hadn't initiated this much touch since the moment I'd seen her after I buried her dog.

After she'd come to my house, I'd taken my fill. Then Allegra had happened.

Yet that didn't mean that I hadn't craved it every day for the last three hundred and forty-seven days. That I hadn't wanted to touch her. To caress her face. To beg for her touch.

The one and only time I'd hugged her—made any more contact than a simple touch—had been the day that she'd given birth to TJ.

The day she'd given me a son. A little person that would carry on the Hail name for the rest of his life.

What I did next was likely the most freeing thing I'd done in my entire life.

I decided to fuck everything. Fuck Allegra. Fuck my brother. Fuck everything that was waiting on me.

Hannah? *Well, fuck her too.*

But I'd be doing it with my body.

The next moment, I showed her.

I stood up, my face even with hers with my legs splayed wide, and I dropped my mouth to hers.

She didn't even hesitate.

She allowed the kiss, and took everything that I gave.

And when I stopped giving? She took it into her own hands, and forced me to continue.

I couldn't say that I was upset about providing that kiss.

I also couldn't say that I was upset when the planter that Allegra had given me 'from Alex' for Father's Day last year fell to the ground and shattered with a sharp crash.

Why? Because that planter hadn't been from Alex. It'd been a reminder from Allegra that she would be watching me.

And honestly, I hoped that she was watching. I hoped that she saw that I was no longer playing her game anymore.

Because the woman in my arms, currently gasping when I shoved her back down to my desk, forcing my hips between her legs, was the woman of my dreams.

She was my *one*.

She was my everything.

Even Allegra hadn't meant the same to me as my woman. Hannah was the one who stayed by me, despite me treating her like trash—and I couldn't say that I didn't do that. I always put my daughter first, and if that meant that the woman that I loved with all my heart got put on the back burner, then so be it.

But, as much as it hurt, I wasn't going to be able to do that anymore.

This was Hannah.

She was the one thing that I could always count on. The woman who, despite my assholeness, stuck by me, and continued to offer me her love, even when I didn't deserve it.

That was changing now.

Now.

Right. Fucking. Now.

I yanked her shirt up and off, exposing those breasts that I'd been longing to feel again. Especially since they'd grown from the moment that we knew about TJ.

She was wearing a nursing bra.

One that was about as unattractive as one could get, but with Hannah? Yeah, she could have no boobs, and I'd still think she was sexy.

But she did have boobs, and the boobs she had were practically spilling out the top and sides.

"God," I groaned.

Before I could reach for her bra, though, she placed her hand on my arm and squeezed.

My eyes met hers.

"Not that I'm not more than willing to do this, but…" She bit her lip, and I knew exactly what she was going to say. "Are you sure?"

I crawled up on the desk with her, making it so that our eyes were directly in line with each other, and told her what was in my heart.

"Have I ever told you I love you?"

Her eyes widened, and instead of answering, she shook her head.

"I do," I murmured. "I've loved you for a long fucking time."

Her eyes closed.

"I love everything about you. Your heart. Your fire. Your girl. Our son. There's not one thing about you that I don't love. Even when you hang your bras up in the bathroom, and forget to put the lid on the toothpaste."

"I know it's sudden. I know that you probably think this is a rash decision on my part, but I'm fucking tired of fighting it. I miss you. I want you in my bed every night. I want to raise our child like he's meant to be raised." I paused. "And if one day Alex plays into that equation, then even better for me. But it hurts. It hurts to see you in my house, and not be able to act on the instincts that urge me to wrap you in my arms."

She cupped my cheek with her small, soft hand.

"I know."

I closed my eyes and dropped my head to her chest, right between those beautiful breasts that were so fucking pretty that it physically hurt.

"But..." she interrupted my musings. "I think that you should talk with Alex...let her know that you're not giving up."

My eyes opened, and they practically blazed.

"I won't ever give up on her," I promised. "But in doing that, I'm not going to give up on you *for* her. Allegra's already proven that she's vindictive enough to do this ten times better than I ever could."

She looked up at the ceiling.

"If we do this, it could literally change everything."

I leaned back to my knees and reached for the front clasp of her bra.

"If we don't do this, it could change everything," I countered.

Then I undid the clasp, and practically salivated all over her as I watched those bountiful breasts pop free.

"I want to taste every inch of you," I told her. "I want to remember everything."

I dropped down and placed a kiss on the tip of each breast.

"I want to learn everything about you, too."

I pressed another kiss to her breastbone.

"I want to lick." I went from one nipple to the other, dragging my tongue as I did. "Are you sensitive here?"

I remembered, very vividly, that she'd been extremely sensitive before, but now, I bet that she was even more so.

"Yes," she hissed, drawing the word out as I circled one nipple with the flat length of my tongue.

She tasted sweet, like milk.

I'd never tasted it before, of course, but there was no other explanation for what that sweetness was.

She confirmed that it was what it was moments later when a tiny white bead pebbled on the tip of one nipple.

My eyes watched it rapturously, and when I bent down, she caught my head in her hand.

"Travis…"

I growled and changed course, detouring to her mouth so I could slam my lips down on hers.

The moment our mouths touched, we went from calm and collected, to heated and out of control.

Her hands went everywhere.

My face. My beard. My shoulders and then my back.

I took what she was willing to give, groaning when she latched onto my neck and bit the cord lightly.

My hardened dick behind my dirty work jeans pressed even more heavily against the unforgiving fly, and with little recourse, I ground it into her pelvis.

I was grateful that she'd spread her legs wide for me which allowed me direct access to the good stuff without much effort.

"Are you sure?" she repeated, this time much more breathlessly.

I growled.

"More than sure."

Then I went for her breast again, this time taking no prisoners when it came to getting that nipple, and that little white drop, in my mouth.

When Allegra was pregnant with Alex, I'd been fascinated by her milk-filled breasts.

When she'd stated her unwillingness to breastfeed our daughter, I didn't complain. I couldn't blame her. It was a whole lot of work, and it wasn't for everybody.

Did that mean I wasn't disappointed, though?

Hell, no. I was extremely disappointed.

I'd always been turned on by it, and now I was about to let that fantasy loose, and I wasn't sure how she'd take it.

But she just watched as I let my tongue go back to that tiny white drop, and swipe it free.

Her eyes only widened slightly, but she cupped my face and brought it back to her mouth.

"Are you really sure?"

I hated to see that hesitation on her face. She wanted this. *I* wanted this. What she nor I wanted was Allegra to freak the fuck out and make this all even worse—which I had no doubt in my mind that she would do.

I'd seen her in action before.

Every single person that crossed the crazy bitch in some way ended up paying—even if it was getting fired from your job where Allegra once tried to return a shirt and been turned away, stating that it was company policy not to accept returns on worn items.

Instead of pursuing it there, she'd then gone to the president of the chain of stores and pleaded her case. Who'd decided to side with Allegra.

Secretly, I was sure that Allegra had probably fucked the man in some way—based on the smile on his face when I'd seen them together—but that was a different story for another day.

Especially when the woman that I'd had a permanent hard-on for was lying on my desk, legs spread wide to accommodate my hips, staring at me like I'd just made all her dreams come true.

"I'm sure."

Then I showed her.

I showed her by touching her.

I showed her by teasing her.

I showed her in each and every kiss. Taste. Touch. Lick.

"Are you really, really sure?"

I ignored her breathy question, instead pressing her breasts together as I tried to lick both nipples at once.

The move caused more breast milk to spill from her nipples, making her gasp.

"Travis…"

The worry in her voice had me smiling, and after licking each drop free, I let her breasts go and moved down, yanking her loose yoga pants down her hips as I went.

"Oh, God."

"Not God, honey. Just me, Travis."

She pulled my hair, causing me to laugh as I paused at the soft swell of her belly.

She had more stretch marks. A lot more.

But they were cute.

Tiny little scars that would forever bear witness of our son's previous position inside of her for a full nine months.

"Beautiful," I told her, then skimmed my lips along the angry looking scar that was healed now, but still very visible.

When Hannah had told me that she wanted to have a vaginal birth after having a C-section, I hadn't realized the danger.

Hadn't realized that it could possibly kill her.

Not until she'd pushed for hours, and was so exhausted that she passed out cold on the hospital bed that she was trying to deliver our son on

CHAPTER 10

Life is like a penis. It gets hard sometimes, but not forever.
-Fact of Life

Travis

63 days ago

I was nervous as hell.

Hannah was exhausted.

She was staring at me, defeat in her eyes, and was crying.

"Baby," I whispered, cupping her cheeks. "You tried so hard…it's okay."

A tear fell from the corner of her eye. "I wanted to do it right."

I smoothed her sweaty hair back from her face.

"You *are* doing it right," I told her.

She took a deep breath, and winced as another contraction took hold.

We'd been at this pushing thing for over four hours. TJ was no closer to coming out now than he was when she'd first started.

I could see the worried looks that the doctor and the nurses were exchanging, and Michael had been back twice to check on her.

Each time he'd left, I could read a little more fear in his eyes.

"Can you get me more ice?"

I nodded, then stood up, walking out moments later with an empty cup.

Michael, Hannah's brother, stopped me the moment that I exited the room.

"Is everything okay?"

I could tell that he was worried. Hell, *I* was worried, and I was in there the whole time.

When Hannah had told us that the only person she wanted in the delivery room was me, rather than her brother and parents who were all in the medical field, I'd been stunned.

Not to mention that I didn't deserve to be there.

But the moment that she'd said it, I'd felt pride in being the first and only one to see our son—at least for a few hours, anyway.

Now, though, I could tell it was taking a toll on everyone else—including her badass brother who hated my guts.

"She's exhausted," I told him bluntly. "She asked for more ice."

Michael swallowed.

"I told her after last time that she shouldn't do this."

My brows furrowed. "What do you mean?"

Michael looked at me, his large, tattooed arms crossed intimidatingly across his chest. "Last time Hannah had to have an emergency C-section due to complications. Complications that the doctor said at the beginning of her pregnancy would likely repeat themselves."

My mouth dropped open.

"What?"

He nodded, letting me know that he was more than serious.

"When was this discussed?"

He just looked at me, and I winced.

I'd missed more than one appointment. It could've been at any of them.

Though, I had made the two biggest ones she'd said—the gender reveal, and the one at twenty-eight weeks when they checked growth.

I felt like my world had just narrowed.

"What can I do now?" I asked, my voice precise and to the point when it was anything but what I was feeling.

Stark terror. Horror. Anger. Dismay.

All of those things were going through me as I asked the man that hated me with a passion, what I was supposed to do.

Michael was an ex-doctor. He'd gone to med school, graduated with his MD, and then had thrown it all away to go into the military—or so Hannah had told me. I hadn't had any interaction with the man due to him despising me, to get any more info, but I trusted him to care for his sister's life.

"Convince her to do the C-section," he told me. "Likely, they'll suggest that soon, anyway, and she's going to expect it."

I looked at the cup of almost-melted ice.

“Okay, I’ll see what I can do.”

I got fresh ice and didn’t once look at Hannah’s brother again, but I felt his eyes on me. Felt his dislike. I knew he thought I was leading his sister on, but I wasn’t.

At least, not intentionally.

And if I were an honest man, I’d admit that I was secretly happy that Hannah hadn’t moved beyond what we’d had. That she hadn’t gone out and found another man.

Hostel, Texas was a small town. Less than ten thousand people in its entirety, but a lot of those residents were unmarried men.

Hostel was what you would call an oil town. Most of its money was made from the oilrigs that lined the outskirts of the city, and those beyond ours. Men were more than prevalent, and it hadn’t gone without notice that Hannah was a beautiful woman. Despite her obvious pregnant state, many men had done their level best to get her to pay attention to them.

It hadn’t worked, thank God.

I’d definitely taken notice, though.

“Oh, God.”

Those two words were muttered the moment that I crossed over the threshold by the doctor.

Which were words that you never wanted to hear leave past their lips when they were supposed to be taking care of the woman that you loved with all your heart—even if she didn’t know it—or if you hadn’t admitted it out loud yet.

“She’s passed out cold,” came the nurse’s voice.

I walked up to the side of the stretcher, doing my best to keep my eyes away from her vaginal area, and walked up to Hannah’s side.

"Is she okay?"

"Exhaustion has set in," came the doctor's reply. "We spoke while you were out of the room about her getting a cesarean. If she's passed out, though, she can't deliver this baby. And the longer the baby stays in the birth canal, the more likely that it'll be that an emergency delivery will be needed."

I glanced up at Hannah's exhausted face, feeling helpless and useless.

"What do we do now?"

"Now, we wait for her to wake back up."

I looked at the man.

"How will we do that?"

"The pain will wake her up shortly. This happens, although not that often," he admitted. "Should have her back here shortly. There's another contraction. It's a monster, too."

Then came Hannah's moan of pain, and her eyelids fluttered open.

The moment that I saw her eyes, I knew that she was mentally and physically depleted, and that this wasn't going to work.

"Honey, we're doing the C-section," I told her bluntly. "Now."

She opened her mouth to protest, but instead a loud sob left her lips.

"I wanted to do this the right way," she wailed, her body curling around her stomach as her body forced her to push despite her exhaustion.

I smoothed her hair out of her face, and dropped my forehead to hers.

"This isn't the wrong way, honey. Not for our baby, and not for you. It's the only way at this point."

She nodded against my forehead, and I leaned back so that I could look at the doctor.

"Let's do the C-section."

The doctor winked at me, but I didn't miss the look of relief that crossed over his features.

Eleven minutes and thirty seconds later, I was watching over the curtain—despite the doctor telling me not to—and holding Hannah's hand as our son was brought into the world.

***

Present day

"Trav?"

Hannah's smooth hands sifted through my hair, and I closed my eyes as I pressed a soft kiss to the scar that looked nothing like it did two months ago.

"You sure?"

In answer, I bit the soft swell of her belly, right above her incision, and growled at her.

I didn't answer her, though. She knew I was sure.

She was trying to give me an out, though.

Little did she know that I didn't want the out. I didn't want to be apart anymore, even when we were so close together.

She started to giggle and pushed my head away, playfully forcing me off of her.

She was bare on my desk moments later, her eyes dilated, and her breath causing her breasts to jump.

"God," I breathed, taking her all in. "You look even more beautiful now than you did the first time I saw you like this."

I had seen her naked in the hospital, of course, but that time I'd tried my level best not to stare during her vulnerable state. I was glad to know that she didn't have a very nasty scar, despite my worries to the contrary.

She reached both hands forward to cover her breasts as I took her in, and I growled and leaned over the desk, putting my face level with hers.

"Don't cover yourself."

"I'm not comfortable with it all hanging out like this," she admitted, gesturing to her body with a vague sweep of her hands.

I could tell.

But little did she know that she was turning me on so much that my balls were seriously about to be permanently blue.

"Does it feel like I don't like the way you look?" I asked, digging my erection into her bare pussy.

She bit her lip and shook her head. "No."

I grinned and leaned back, taking off my shirt by hooking a single finger in the back of the collar and hunching over while I pulled it from my body.

She watched avidly as I did, her eyes taking everything in all at once.

I didn't miss the look she gave my crotch shortly after.

"You want my pants off, too?"

She nodded without uttering a word.

I took my belt off and let it fall to the floor, following that up by yanking open the button of my pants.

She moaned low in her throat as the lowered zipper caused my pants to gape, giving her the first good look at my commando state.

The only thing she could really see was the base of my cock and my pubic hair, but it was enough of a glimpse to cause her to bite her lip and stare up at me with a look of pleading in her eyes.

Whether that look was a plea to have me take her, or for her to suck it, I didn't know.

But I chose to take it as her wanting to suck it, so I walked around the desk and let my jeans fall to the floor.

My cock sprang free only inches from her mouth, causing her to lean forward and capture just the crown in less time than it took for me to get my footing.

Footing that was very important to standing when you had a woman like Hannah sucking on your cock.

The moment her mouth closed over the sensitive tip, I had to reach for the edge of the desk by her head to keep myself from falling on top of her and choking her with it.

Though, the way she was going down on me, up and down the length of my shaft, had me doubting that it would bother her.

Then she moved, allowing her head to fall completely off the desk, and I realized only seconds later what she was after.

"You want me to…"

She pulled off of me. "Fuck my mouth."

Then she leaned backward again and opened her mouth, inviting me in a way only a woman as sensual as Hannah could do.

The moment that I sank my cock partially inside of her, a rough curse left my lips.

The second time, when she took three quarters of me, another one spilled forth.

"Oh, fuck me." I squeezed the corner of the desk harder, white knuckling it as I tried to find the ability to breathe.

It was as if she were sucking everything out of me, though, making it to where I couldn't breathe, let alone think of words to say that didn't start with the letter F.

"Fuck," I growled, unsure what I was asking for. "Fuck me."

My hands dropped down to her bouncing breasts as I fucked her mouth, and suddenly I couldn't handle it anymore.

I had to be inside of her.

Pulling out of her so abruptly that she gasped in surprise, I rounded the desk and crawled up onto the desk between her legs.

Lining my cock up with her entrance, I at first eased inside.

When it was evident that she was just as tight as she'd been the first time, I realized that doing anything slow was out of the question. I hadn't had sex for a year, and hadn't jacked off in well over six months. Hence why I slammed inside her.

She gasped and lifted her hips, practically begging me to do anything I could to make the ache between her legs go away.

"Ah, fuck." I strained my head backward as I felt the warmth of heaven wrapped around my cock. "Jesus Christ, yes."

The slide in and out of her was so monumental that I couldn't find words to express the gloriousness of the feeling.

And when she started to ripple around me, signaling her orgasm after only a few strokes on my part, I clutched onto her thigh as it rocked me.

"Oh, God. Oh, God. Oh, God." Hannah's nipples pebbled, and more than a drop spilled from her breasts this time.

My eyes were so transfixed on the flow that I didn't realize how close I was to my breaking point until I felt the come boiling in my balls and rising up my shaft.

That was about the time that my phone rang, and I knocked it over.

My orgasm rushed through me, and I cursed as I finally realized exactly what I'd done.

I'd fucked her bare.

Again.

Jesus Christ.

There was just something about Hannah's pussy that made my mind go blank. Turned me stupid.

Did that stop me from coming inside of her, though? *No.*

Did it stop me from thinking about how nice it would be to have another kid with her? *Again, a big resounding no.*

And as each pulse left me in a wet, hot stream and deposited inside of her, I knew that there wasn't anything in the world I cared about but this. Now. Us. Her.

Not anything.

And even when I heard someone speaking on the phone that'd overturned, I still did nothing.

CHAPTER 11

Today, be the badass girl you were too lazy to be yesterday.
-Coffee Cup

Hannah

Present day

I hadn't been sure that I'd ever feel happy again. Not truly.

Sure, I had a son that was my world, and a daughter that was the light of my life. But with all that God had blessed me with, I still wanted more. And that more was the man that had just made love to me on the desk in his office.

We stared at each other, both of us still breathing hard, as we digested what we'd just done.

"Travis…" I hesitated.

He leaned forward, his cock still inside of me, and pressed his forehead to mine.

"Don't," he whispered. "This is one of the best days of my life."

My world shimmered as tears started to form in my eyes.

"You…"

He closed my mouth with his, stopping the words before they left my lips.

"I'm tired of fighting."

I blinked, letting the first tear fall.

He kissed it away with his mouth.

"Allegra doesn't have any place with us anymore."

Normally I would've balked at hearing another woman's name roll off a man's lips when he was still hard and buried inside of me. But this time? Those words were like music to my ears.

"But Alex…"

He dropped his forehead back to mine.

"I can't dance to Allegra's tune anymore," he told me, blunt honesty written all over his face. "It hurts like my heart is being ripped straight out of my chest, but she's already done that damage with me and Alex. If there's anything left, I'll repair it. But, to be honest, she's going to have to be older before she understands that I'm not the bad guy."

"But that could take years!" I cried.

He smiled sadly.

"I've done everything right. I've paid my child support. Contacted a lawyer. She's not breaking any of the rules. She's only filling my child with lies. I've tried to get full custody of her, but Allegra's not technically a bad mother…it's only in my eyes—and likely yours—that she's doing anything 'bad.' No court in the state of Texas will take her away from Allegra."

I knew that.

It hurt, but I knew that.

I knew it well.

I'd watched Travis struggle with the fact over the last year, and each time his daughter said that she hated him, it broke something inside of me.

"Trav…"

He kissed me breathless. "I'll still get her. I'll see her. I'll try my hardest…but I'll do it with you at my side."

Those words had been the ones that I wanted to hear…I just didn't like that he'd had to hit rock bottom with his daughter to say them.

I thought that those words would never come. That I'd never see the end.

And now that he was telling me everything that I wanted to hear, I wasn't sure that I could trust them.

It'd been a long time, but this last year, with Travis only giving half of himself to me, I wasn't sure that I'd ever find a way to be happy again.

And now that it was within sight, I wasn't sure that I could trust it.

But I owed it to my kids to try.

I owed it to myself.

I deserved happiness.

And, so did Travis.

"Travis?"

Someone knocked on the door, and I froze.

"Who is that?" I hissed.

"The receptionist I hired last week. The one that has the hots for every man in the office." He reminded me of what he'd told me last week.

He'd said that she was a young girl with stars in her eyes, and dreams of snagging herself a man.

Well, this was one man that she wouldn't be snagging.

"Get up," I told him, patting his shoulder.

He did, pulling out seconds later.

I winced at the wet feeling, but wasn't alarmed. At my six-week exam, I had an IUD placed. Granted, I hadn't thought that I was going to use it as fast as I had, which was a mere two weeks from when I'd had it put in, but it was what it was.

And I was glad that I got it.

As much as I loved my son and daughter, having kids was a huge pain in the ass when you had to work full time to support yourself.

Before I could so much as roll up on Travis' desk, I found myself hoisted up by the hips and placed on my sock-covered feet.

I wiggled my toes and looked at the hole that was in one sock, right above my middle toe, and winced.

Today hadn't been about looking sexy.

I was tired, exhausted, and had TJ's two-month checkup—which was why I was off of work at all.

Today's visit to Hail Auto Recovery had been about telling Travis how TJ had practically bounded to the top of the growth and height charts at the doctors, and it had turned into this.

Not that I wasn't happy with where it had gone, because I sure as hell was. And so was my vagina.

But damn, if I'd known, I would've worn something sexier than what I had.

Speaking of clothes, my shirt smacked me in my face, and my yoga pants hit me somewhere below the waist and fell to my feet.

I glared at the man that'd thrown them at me, and reached down to snap my bra back into place.

That was when I saw the mess that I'd made.

Well, fuck.

There was breast milk all over my chest, and still leaking out, might I add.

But, with nothing else to do, I closed the bra anyway, thankful that I had those little cup things in that caught all the overflow, and shrugged into my shirt.

I was just reaching for my panties that were tangled in my pants when the door was pushed open.

"I'm tired of waiting, Travis Hail."

I froze behind Travis' desk, so very thankful that it was one of those huge ones that blocked everything—otherwise The Devil—also known as Travis' ex-wife—would've gotten more than she bargained for.

Here we go.

Travis' words were about to be put to the test a lot sooner than he'd thought.

The moment that her eyes came to a rest on me, I dropped my hands in hopes of hiding my nearly naked state.

"Hello, Allegra." I smiled, wondering if my hair was a mess.

It probably was.

It hadn't been all that great to begin with thanks to the fact that my straightener pooped out that morning. In my hurry to get out the door, I'd thrown it up into a braid and called it done.

I could feel wisps around my face, and I knew that I looked a little unkempt.

Hopefully, though, I didn't look sexed up like I was feeling.

Then I started to worry.

The room had to smell like sex. Jizz had a distinct smell, and sometimes so did a vagina.

But then I remembered the fan that was in the corner of the room, always running.

Travis couldn't function without a fan—something about him hating stale, stagnant air.

When I'd gone to ask him about always having one pointed at him, he'd only shrugged saying that it was a comfort thing. However, thanks to whatever phobia he wouldn't talk about, I knew that the room wouldn't smell too bad.

"Shouldn't you be at work?" she hissed.

My brows rose, and I decided to take a seat in the chair and scoot up underneath the desk just in case she came any further into the room. If she did, she'd see that I wasn't currently wearing pants, and I wasn't sure how that would go down due to how much Allegra already disliked me.

"Allegra."

Travis' words had a bite to them that I'd never heard him use with her before.

I kinda liked it!

"Well, you're the asshole that invited me here. How about you tell me why you called?" She dismissed me completely, not bothering to wait for me to answer her.

Travis, who I now saw, was completely dressed.

Guess that was a plus to our hurried frenzy moments earlier.

Thank God.

"Actually, I called to tell you that we needed to talk about the visitation schedule coming up," he said. "With summer coming, I'd like to discuss taking Alex for a full month stretch. Allowing you to have her the complete month of July. I want to go camping in the RV with my parents, and I'd really like to take her with me."

I'd get up and leave if I wouldn't draw attention to myself. I was fairly positive Allegra would notice that I was half naked.

Oh, and let's not forget the fact that I was now dripping with him.

"Absolutely not," Allegra growled. "She will not spend a month straight with you. There's no telling how she'll act when she comes back from that."

Or how much better she'll act, but who was I to say anything?

"I heard that your father will be leaving for Europe in July. You were wanting to go with him."

Allegra didn't say anything to that.

"You're not allowed to take her out of the state without my permission," Travis continued on. "And I won't be giving that if you don't allow me to have her for the full month that we're camping."

Allegra looked like she'd stuck her tongue into something vile.

"Will *she* be there?"

Allegra's words were curt, and I wanted to throat punch her.

"No," I denied. "I need to work to pay my bills. I can't just take a month off," I snapped, hating her with every freakin' ounce of my body.

If there were a word that was more severe than despise, or loathe, then that would be what I felt for the woman.

That vindictive, only caring about herself, woman.

Allegra didn't have to work to pay her bills. Travis did it for her. Alimony in the form of six hundred dollars a month, not to mention six hundred dollars a month in child support.

Though, I guess I should be more thankful that it wasn't more. Travis had been to court eight months ago when Allegra had decided that twelve hundred dollars a month wasn't enough for her to live on—despite living with her parents and not having to pay a single thing—unlucky for her, she'd ended up having her alimony reduced from twelve hundred bucks a month to six hundred. Then, when she wasn't satisfied with the court's orders, she'd tried to get more child support. That time, there was a woman judge that was known to side with the woman on most cases, and the child support went from three hundred forty a month to four hundred.

So, he'd received a tally for the win column, and a tally for the loss column. Regardless, he still had to pay her money each month that she didn't deserve, especially when she was living somewhere that didn't require a rent check every month. She had a fairly new car that was paid off, also. Travis bought all of Alex's clothes—which I would know since I bought them at the same time as I bought Reggie's clothes. Though, Travis paid me back for it ninety nine percent of the time.

So no, she really had no expenses and had no clue what it was like to have to work for a living seeing as she hadn't worked a day in her life.

Her father had supported her from the day she was born to the day she turned twenty-two, and Travis had done it after that. When they'd gotten divorced, Allegra had moved straight back into her parents' house, and Travis still cut her checks every month.

I, on the other hand, had lived by myself for four years before I'd met my ex, and then when we divorced two years after Reggie was born, I'd lived by myself since.

I'd bought all of my own cars. I paid my own health and car insurance. I was a big freakin' girl with big girl freakin' panties. Allegra was a spoiled rotten brat that likely didn't wear any panties at all.

"Do you mind leaving?" Allegra asked me.

I looked over at Travis, giving him my 'I don't know what to do' look.

He winked at me.

"Hannah is my fiancée, and deserves to hear everything that's being said," he interjected. "I'm sorry, but she's not leaving."

My mouth literally dropped open in surprise, and I stared at the man who'd just uttered words I never thought would leave his lips.

"She's your what?" Allegra shrieked.

I, however, was too busy trying to gather my bearings.

Fiancée? Deserves to hear whatever Allegra had to say. What?

I hadn't missed that during my twenty-two minutes and thirty-nine seconds in this room…*had I?*

No, I was fairly positive I'd remember being asked to marry someone, and Travis wasn't good enough to cause me to lose my mind quite that far.

Sure, he was excellent. Tongue tangling, for sure. What he wasn't was one who got off on making me speak in tongues—or speaking in tongues altogether.

No, I would've remembered.

"Fiancée," Travis repeated. "We're getting married next year, but no, since she can't get off of work, she'll be unable to go on the RV with us. That's not to say she won't drive to those places and meet us for a few days."

Oh really?

Allegra's hard, cold eyes cut to me, and then moved back to Travis.

"Over my dead body will you get to take her with that woman."

I gritted my teeth.

This was exactly how it was with Allegra.

They'd been divorced for seven years when I came along, and had been separated for nearly a year before their divorce. So, in no way, shape, or form was this a new thing when I came into the picture.

Yet, Allegra always acted like she had some previous claim on Travis, and made it very clear that nobody would have him but her.

In all honesty, it was exhausting.

There were days that I wished I'd never met Travis.

Then I immediately began to feel bad because if I hadn't met Travis, I wouldn't have my son. And Travis wouldn't have me.

Travis needed the proof that not all women were vindictive like his ex.

"Well, then we can agree to disagree that you will be taking my child to Europe with you. So unless you're willing to stay behind—which I highly doubt that you are—you'll have to agree to those terms."

Allegra's cold, dark gray eyes were positively glacial when she swept her gaze over the two of us.

"You'll regret this. Both of you."

Travis shook his head. "There's not a single thing when it comes to you, that I don't regret."

Allegra's mouth dropped open.

"You can't mean that," she said. "Alex…"

Travis didn't say a word.

I knew in his heart that he didn't regret Alex. But Alex had been the baby that had trapped Travis with Allegra. The final straw that broke the camel's back, so to speak.

And now that kid was acting like her father—who loved her with all his heart despite the beginning of how she came to be—was an annoying gnat to be shooed away.

She was Allegra's new mini-me.

And I hated that. I hated it bad. Yet there wasn't a single thing I could do about it.

Travis stared at Allegra, and finally she opened the door.

"You'll need to realize that you're not the only person in this town that can do the things you do."

Travis raised a brow at her.

"Are you threatening me or my business?" he asked, sounding mildly curious.

"If you want to take it that way," she sniffed. "Have a pleasant day…Travis."

With that, the woman left, not once looking back.

Travis said something quietly to someone beyond the door—likely his new receptionist—and slammed the door shut.

I stayed where I was, wondering if Travis locked it or not. Because I wasn't going to go pantless in front of anybody else.

"Can you stand there and make sure that nobody else comes in?" I asked him when he started around the desk.

He grinned and winked, his eyes going to his destroyed desk—which I was just now seeing—and back to me. "I locked it…unlike you."

I lifted my lip at him in a silent snarl. "I didn't know that you were going to…" I dropped my voice down to the barest of whispers, "fuck me."

He started to laugh, even going as far as to lean his left hand against the desk as he bent over and guffawed.

"Hannah, honey." He grinned at me, and it sent shivers down my spine to see him smile at me with such happiness. "There are no kids here. You don't have to whisper the curse words."

I shrugged and stood up, pulling my underwear on, followed shortly by my pants.

The last thing to go on were my flip-flops.

"I have to go," I growled. "I have a doctor's appointment in thirty minutes. I haven't gone to the grocery store yet, and I need to get Reggie's family tree ready."

He held up his hand. "What family tree?"

I frowned. "I told you last week that both girls had family trees. You were supposed to call your mom."

He threw his head back and growled at the ceiling. "I forgot."

I winked at him.

"I know. Which is why I called her last week when you only gave me a nod instead of doing it right then."

Travis' mom and I got along famously, and everyone loved me.

At first it was incredibly awkward to love a man that refused to return those feelings, and love his parents and family just as much as you loved your own. But now, it was as if they'd always been there, and I adored them.

Before I could exit like I'd originally intended to do, he hooked me around the waist and brought me around to face him.

"I know that me telling you that I was ready to make this work, and that I loved you, isn't enough. I know that you're going to need time from me, and I'm willing to give that to you." He paused. "You've been there through everything over the last year. You've stayed when any other woman would've run. I owe you so much, but I'm going to keep asking you for more. I'm going to take, and take, and take, until you don't think you have anything left to give. Then, when I'm sure I have it all, I'm going to marry you. Tie you to me forever, and make sure you don't ever want to leave. I'm going to treat you the way you deserve to be treated, and I won't fuck this up. I might, upon occasion, do something stupid. But just know that if I do, I'll always make it up to you."

Those words might've sounded stalkerish coming from anyone else. Coming from Travis, though, with his eyes locked on mine?

Not nearly as scary.

"Okay," I whispered.

He dropped his forehead to mine, breathed me in for a few long seconds, and then let me go with a soft kiss to the tip of my nose.

"Be careful."

My smile was brilliant.

"Yes, sir."

He winked. "Now you got it right."

I rolled my eyes and left, doing what I said I was going to do.

What I hadn't expected when I got to my staff meeting, however, was to be fired.

CHAPTER 12

There should be a calorie refund for things that didn't taste as good as expected.
-Coffee Cup

Travis

I pulled up to the house, took a short look around to ascertain that I was alone, and pulled the wheel hard to the left. Making sure I was in a good position, I backed the tow truck up to the car that was sitting in the middle of the driveway—in a seedy part of Hostel—and got out.

My eyes quickly dashed around the area, noting that there were three people that I could see out on the porches of various houses, and of the three people, only one looked like he gave more than one shit that I was taking possession of a car by force.

Keeping my eye on him out of the corner of my eye, I got all the hooks, cables, and chains attached to the car, and then started to tighten them.

By the time that the back end of the car I was sent to repossess by the bank was safely hitched up onto my tow truck, only five minutes had passed.

However, it was the sound of the winch working that made the right amount of noise to alert the man in the house who owned this particular car.

"Hey!"

I finished locking the car into place and rounded the back of the truck.

I'd just opened the door and was lifting my leg inside when the man rounded the hood of the truck and slammed his hands down on the door.

It closed right on my leg, but I didn't let on that it hurt.

"Can I help you?" I questioned calmly.

If I'd responded with anything else, I knew from experience that I'd be sparking the man's ire—even more than I already had.

"That's my car. Put it down."

I shook my head. "It may be your car, but since the note hasn't been paid on it in over four months, the bank that you purchased the loan from is legally free to take it back. Which they've done."

"You can't do that!" he screamed.

And then he started to reach for his pants.

I chose that moment to slam the door shut, wincing when the first bullet ricocheted off the bulletproof glass that Dante and I had decided to splurge on.

It'd cost us a fucking mint to put it into five new trucks, but at this point, as I looked at the bullet that would've gone straight into my goddamn chest, I was grateful that we'd spent it.

And as the next shot bounced off right around where my head would've been, I said a prayer.

"Shots fired," I heard over the radio in the truck.

I was linked into the police ban of the county, and although we no longer had a local police department, we did have a sheriff.

A sheriff that had bigger fish to fry most times then to come patrol the tiny town of Hostel.

'Shots fired' however, was going to get the Sheriff, as well as any law enforcement within a twenty-minute radius to head toward the shooting.

The volunteer fire department would've also answered the call, but since the shooter was still firing at the truck—surely, he'd be out of bullets soon—they couldn't come any closer until he was contained.

But when he reached into his pocket and produced another magazine, I realized that this man would literally fire at me for hours if I continued to just sit here.

Which was why I chose to do what I did next—leave.

The man apparently had been anticipating that I'd do it, because the moment the truck went into gear, he threw himself at the car before it could pass.

He yanked the car's door that I'd had hooked up to the truck open, and launched himself inside head first.

I looked at the ceiling and called into dispatch, using my own code that the sheriff's department had given The 'Hail Raisers' as he'd dubbed us early on in Dante's and my tenure.

"Dispatch, this is 0224 requesting backup to 20029 Boddy Road. I have a white male trying to remove his car from my possession."

"10-4, 0224. Backup is on the way."

I rehung the microphone and stared in my rearview mirror for all of ten seconds before I pulled my phone out of my pocket and started to browse Pinterest.

Don't ask me why I was cruising Pinterest. Honestly, it was Hannah's fault. I'd been a Pinterest virgin before Hannah had come into my life, and ruined me.

While I was cruising 'old collectible cars' my mother called. I winced, wondering if she would call back immediately if I ignored it, and decided that yes. Yes, she fucking would.

So I bit the bullet and answered it.

"Hey, Ma," I greeted her.

A jolt had me glancing up to the rearview mirror as I watched the man try to drive his car off of my truck. With the back end suspended by the frame, and the only thing with purchase being the front tires, I had no doubt that he wouldn't be able to go anywhere.

But to be sure, I lifted the front end just a little bit higher, allowing only about an inch of tire to touch the pavement.

"Hey, sugar," my momma said. "What time can I expect you and Hannah for dinner tonight?"

I looked at my watch and contemplated telling her no.

I knew better, though. She'd hold dinner until midnight if she had to. Then my father would call me all pissed off because he was made to wait, and I'd never hear the end of it.

"I don't know…"

"Finley and Leida are here for the weekend. I'd count it as a favor if you deigned to grace us with your presence. I already know that Hannah, the girls, and TJ will be coming."

I winced, remembering that Alex would be there tonight. I'd forgotten that she was coming, which instantly made me feel like shit.

What I loved, though, was that she had no problem speaking directly to Hannah.

They had a special relationship, and had from the very start.

The first day that my mother had met Hannah had been the day that Hannah had come to my office to tell me that she was pregnant. It'd all been rather awkward, and to be honest, I was fairly sure that my mother fell in love with Hannah, right then and there.

***

250 days ago

"Thanks for lunch, Mom," I murmured softly. "Are you okay?"

My mom looked every single one of her sixty-six years, and she hadn't used to. She was a farmer's wife, and later a businessman's wife. She'd always aged well, but the passing of Dante's wife and children, as well as my sister taking her life, had taken its toll on her.

She wasn't the same smiling woman that she used to be, and I could understand why.

It didn't mean that it hurt any less to see.

"I'm okay, baby." She smiled. "I'm heading to see Tobias and Finley this weekend. Was there anything you wanted me to take to them?"

I shook my head. "I sent the stuff I had for Tobias in the mail last week. He got it and sent it back to me already."

She nodded, her eyes taking on a faraway look as her eyes focused on Dante's empty office door.

"How's Dante?"

I didn't have any good news for her. What Dante was, was not good. In fact, if there was one thing he was, it was a mess.

"He'll get there, Ma," I soothed.

I didn't mention that my brother had gotten rip roaring drunk two weeks ago and fucked some random woman he'd met at the club, and then had skipped town the next day.

Though, it wouldn't be long before she knew.

Especially since that same girl was the same woman who was the hostess at the club for a little over a month—that was before Dante had broken her with whatever he'd said or did. She wasn't a gossip by any means. In fact, she was so quiet, I never would've expected her to go for Dante in the first place.

She'd lived across the street from me for a little over two months before she'd shown up for a job interview. The man in charge of hiring hadn't known the connection to me, and had taken her on with exuberance because we were so short staffed.

It would only be later, when Dante was taking her home and showing up at my house the next day hungover as hell asking for a ride, when we realized who exactly she was.

Regardless of what Dante had done, it was a big fucking mess. She knew that Dante was in no place to be doing what they did, and she showed that by leaving the very next day. Everyone in the entire freakin' town had known about Dante. Everyone, including her.

We hadn't seen her since.

"I hope so," she whispered, voice shaking. "I miss them so much. It's so hard not being able to kiss them. I miss waking them up from their nap and having baby girl ask me to bake something."

Baby girl was what my mother called Dante's eldest. She was the second grandchild in the family, and since Leida, her first grandchild, didn't live here, she'd been the most spoiled. Then came along Dante's baby, and my mother was in love.

From the moment Dante and his wife had returned to work after having her, my mother had watched them instead of them being taken to daycare.

Now, my mother had time on her hands, and she used that time to think about the things that she could no longer change. Now she used most of her free time to bother me, and visit with our other brothers who lived a couple of hours east.

"I know you do, Mom," I grunted and stood, wrapping my arms around her. She was smaller than the last time I did this. "You need to eat more."

She started to laugh a watery laugh, and my belly clenched.

"I want you to find a woman, Travis," she whispered. "I want you…"

A knock came at my door, and I looked up to see Tate Casey standing there. "You have a visitor."

I looked past Tate's shoulder to see Hannah shifting from foot to foot nervously.

Then, her face went pale, and she slapped a hand over her mouth.

My body clenched as I made a move toward Hannah, but before I could so much as let my mother go, she was running toward the front door of the building.

I let my mother go and cursed as I ran after her, coming to a stop outside just as Hannah bent over the flowerbed that my mother had insisted we put in 'for aesthetics' and lost her lunch.

"Hannah…" I paused. "You okay?"

She squatted down and placed her hands over the back of her neck. "I'm pregnant. You got me pregnant."

A gasp left my lips, as well as my mother's, who I hadn't realized had followed me out.

"Come again?" I blinked.

She looked at me, leaving her hands on her neck where they were, and nodded miserably. "Yep. You heard right."

"Oh, my God," my mother cried, sounding happy, but trying to act like she wasn't.

I was too flabbergasted to reply to either Hannah's words, or my mother's.

Instead, I walked to the huge fucking rock that my mother had insisted we put there in the flowerbed and took a seat, directly next to Hannah's stomach contents.

"When did you find out?"

She pushed up and then back, coming to her ass on the sidewalk. "I'm so sorry."

She looked at my mother, as well as Tate Casey who didn't even try to make it look like he wasn't paying attention, and then back to me.

I waved her worry away. "That's my mother and Tate Casey. They both know me well. It's not a big deal that they know…"

She dropped her head and sighed.

"To answer your question, I've been trying to work up the courage to tell you for a week now."

Then, to add the icing to the cake, Allegra chose that time to pull into the parking lot—fifteen minutes early to drop Alex off for her weekend with me—and got out.

"Son of a bitch," I muttered darkly.

Hannah looked up, followed my gaze to the parking lot, and stiffened.

I wasn't sure if she knew the woman getting out of the car, but this was a fairly small town. Allegra was on fucking commercials for her father—who was a used car salesman. She was well known, and still sometimes used my last name because she thought it was funny to torture me.

"Grandma!" Alex cried out. "Hey!"

Alex, my lovely daughter, came running over and threw herself into my mother's arms.

My mother gobbled the attention up, sending me a gloating look. One that I returned. Only, my look was one of annoyance.

Alex wasn't my biggest fan since her mother and I had split, and Allegra had a lot to do with that. She loved my mother, though.

My mother obviously didn't realize how much Alex disliked being with me, otherwise I was sure she wouldn't have looked so smug. She didn't like seeing her babies hurting.

Alex was a very intuitive child. One that knew that just last year, her mother and I had been together and what she thought was happy. Now it was all my fault that we were no longer together, and I had no doubt in my mind that Alex heard that from Allegra on a daily basis.

"Hey, Alex. How you doin', baby?" my mother cried.

Hannah started to look green around the gills again, and I prayed that she would be able to hold it together while Allegra was here.

My luck was that she wouldn't and Allegra would find out, then things would get even worse.

The good thing was that Hannah *was* able to keep it together. The bad thing was that apparently, Hannah hadn't been discreet buying her pregnancy test, and Allegra was already aware of the rumors surrounding the new girl. (Like I said, this was a small town, and people loved to gossip.)

What Allegra hadn't been aware of was who had gotten the new girl pregnant.

Now, seeing the two of us so close, she put two and two together.

And what I saw in Allegra's eyes was enough to make my stomach sour.

"Well, well, well," Allegra drawled.

The words weren't sing-song. They were sharp and hard. Like a fucking knife.

God. Dammit.

CHAPTER 13

I like to make lists. I also like to leave them on the kitchen table and guess what I need when I'm at the store.
-Hannah's secret thoughts

Hannah

Present day

I should've known that it was too good to be true.

The bad things started happening the first day after Travis told Allegra how it was going to be, and it started with his daughter.

I was with Travis when we went to pick her up from the parking lot of The Dollar Store where they always met for the exchange.

I should've known when Alex got out—on her own volition this time instead of having to be taken out kicking and screaming by Travis—that it was going to be bad.

Alex walked over to the car like she didn't have a care in the world. She had her backpack on one shoulder, and a smile on her face.

She got into the truck, didn't complain once about having to sit next to TJ like she normally did, and even set her bag down carefully without jostling the baby or the car seat as she did.

I looked over at Travis as he waited for Alex to buckle the seatbelt, and widened my eyes.

He shook his head, feeling about the same as me that this was a rare phenomenon, and shrugged.

The drive all the way to dinner was nerve wracking as we both waited for the other shoe to drop.

But it never did. Not then. Not fifteen minutes into dinner. Not when Leida went up to Alex and gave her a hug—they were nearly the same age, and had been the best of friends since they both were born.

"I'm glad that she's back," Travis' mother, Allora, mused. "It's nice to have her talking and being friendly instead of sitting in a corner and spitting at us when we get too close."

I winced.

I hadn't actually been here for any of their interactions for a while—at least a couple months before TJ was born. So this was news hearing that Alex was less than nice. At least to her grandmother, that was.

Not that it surprised me.

Alex was *that* kid. The one that you hated but loved at the same time.

I couldn't help but love her. She was part of Travis. A huge part of him that he loved with all of his heart, so how could I not love her?

But being her friend had not happened. She'd scorned every and any attempt that I'd made to get to know her. I bought her presents. Clothes. Took her to see movies. I was the best friend that everyone loved—but Alex. Alex hated me, and made no attempt to hide that fact.

"Fuckin' breath of fresh air," Colder, Travis' father, grunted. "Was starting to think there was something wrong with her."

"It was like coming back to night and day," Evander, an employee and friend of Travis, muttered. "I went to jail for four years. When I'd left, she was always giving hugs, and warm. Then I got back, and it was like the kid had been switched with her alternate alien version. I don't think I've gotten a single hug since I've been back."

Kennedy, Evander's wife, curled up to his side. "Well, four years is a long time for a child. They grow up, change, and move on. It's very possible that she is a different kid, at least in the knowledge sense. She's more able to comprehend the things that go on around her."

I.e., the divorce, and her parents no longer being together. Not to mention the fact that I'd had a baby with her father.

Yeah, those kinds of things.

"Whatever the reason, I'm just glad she's not spitting at you. That shit drives me insane, and I want to spank her ass. But you damn well know the minute you do anything to her, her mother is going to report it to the cops. The kid could use a good ass whoopin'," Colder muttered.

I couldn't agree more, yet I couldn't do a damn thing about it.

"Did you see that Allegra's in another commercial?" Baylor asked, sidling into the conversation, taking a seat, and deftly removing a sleeping TJ from his mother's arms. "This one was for a 'darn good deal.' She even spread out the cash like she used to."

Allegra Levaux was Hostel royalty. Her father owned a chain of car lots, and was richer than Elvis—as well as more popular around here.

"Yeah, it was annoying as fuck," Baylor continued when nobody spoke. "She does this wave and dance that lifts her skirt up. Looks like a total hoochie."

I didn't reply, trying not to get sucked into this 'trash Allegra' business that Travis' family always fell into the moment that they could. I *tried* not to do that. Maybe because I wouldn't want anyone else to do it to me, and also, because Alex always seemed to know when someone was talking bad about her shitty mom. Like now.

She was staring at us from where she was sitting outside, watching, but not moving.

"You have company," I gestured toward Alex. "Let's not talk about this. I swear, it feels like that kid has super hearing or something. She always knows when her mother is being talked about—like a sixth sense or something."

Baylor said something under his breath and changed the subject.

"So, are you and Trav going to have any more babies?"

I looked at Baylor in surprised.

"Uhh, no," I said. "We have three total together. It's simpler if we just deal with what we have. That, and I'm not a good pregnant person. I gained fifty pounds, and I'm still carrying twenty-five of it around on my hips two months later."

Allora snorted. "I'm carrying around fifty pounds thirty years later. You have no worries."

Baylor snorted. "You popped out eight kids. You look damn good for that."

I agreed. Allora and Colder had six boys and two girls, all of which were over ten pounds each. She did damn good.

Travis passed by the window, ruffled Leida's hair, and went to Reggie. She was sitting on the swing set, pumping her little legs to carry her higher and higher.

Then my heart leapt into my throat as she launched herself out of the swing.

Travis caught her, but that didn't make my heart feel any better.

"Jesus Christ," I muttered, looking away from Reggie, who was laughing hysterically and already running back toward the swing set. My best guess, to do it again.

But by averting my eyes, I inadvertently dropped them down to Alex, who was watching her father with such a look of longing that it made me freeze.

The others around us, however, continued talking about a football game that was coming on in an hour, and didn't see the devastated little girl.

I sure did, though.

And when Baylor walked outside with a now awake TJ and offered him to Travis so he could capture Leida and swing her up into his arms, I didn't miss the look Alex gave Travis' back, again.

It was one of anger, resentment, and calculation.

***

Seven hours later, at two in the morning, I heard a soft thump.

My brows furrowing, I got up, thinking that it'd been a little bit longer than TJ normally went between feedings, and started down the hall to TJ's room.

I'd just pushed the door open when I saw a form standing over TJ's bed.

I flipped on the lights and saw Alex, standing on a chair, glaring down at TJ.

The moment the light flicked on, Alex turned and I saw the hatred there.

"Alex, what are you doing?"

She looked so much like her mother that it kind of sickened me a little.

Not that I'd ever admit as much. Travis didn't need to hear or know my inner musings.

"I hate him."

I blinked.

"Alex…"

"I hate you, too."

That I knew.

"I wish you would die."

My jaw worked. "But he's a baby, and I don't wish he would die. I wish he weren't born, though. Every single day."

I walked further into the room and closed the door behind me, then walked up to the chair that I used to rock TJ while I nursed him in the middle of the night.

"Alex," I paused, looking at her. "I know you don't like me."

Her eye twitched.

"But what I don't understand is why you would hate a baby. He's done nothing to you. But if you gave him a chance, you might actually like him."

"He's the reason that my mommy and daddy will never be back together."

There were so many things wrong with that statement that I didn't know where to begin.

"Your mommy and daddy were divorced for an entire two years before TJ came into the picture, baby," I told her softly. "They were never going to get back together."

Her eyes flared with anger.

"My mommy told me that they were, and that if you weren't there telling Daddy you would hurt me, that he would be with her right now."

Oh, God.

That woman.

That fucking woman.

What a bitch!

"Alex, sweetheart." I leaned forward. "I would never, ever do that."

She tossed me an unbelieving glare and climbed down from the stool.

Of course, when she did, she accidentally knocked it against the bed, causing TJ to wake up.

Knowing the moment that his eyes opened that he'd need to eat, I went ahead and picked him up, changed him, and used the time with my back to the little girl to plan out what I was going to say next.

I didn't say another word until I was in the chair and feeding him.

She just watched me with narrowed eyes, her smart little brain taking in everything at once.

"My mommy says that is disgusting. We saw you doing it at your job the other day, and Mommy said that she was very offended by watching you."

Well, then.

"Your mommy had the option to feed you like that, but chose not to. Every woman gets the same choice. Some choose to, and some choose not to," I told her.

Why I'd taken the time to explain it all to her, I didn't know.

She was likely too young to comprehend what that meant, but I didn't bother pausing as I explained.

"Breasts are made to nourish a child," I explained as I rocked. "Not all women breastfeed, but a lot do. I do. Not because I'm all gung ho on breastfeeding, but because it's cheaper."

That was really the reason.

I hated the idea of spending forty dollars a can on formula. If I could save money by feeding him like nature intended for him to be fed, then that's what I would do.

"What?" Alex asked. "Mommy said…"

Gently I explained to her the art of breastfeeding, and then she started to ask questions. All during this process, not once did she snarl, get angry, or say anything discourteous at all.

It was actually quite nice to speak to Alex instead of having her be ugly.

"Your daddy and I were talking about going to Disneyland this summer," I told her. "We've already discussed the benefits of staying there, rather than just visiting for the day. If you were to go, would you want to stay there, or maybe stay at the beach?"

Technically we were going to do both, but I liked talking to her without the nasty words thrown in. It was therapeutic in a way.

"I'd rather go to Disneyland than the beach," she said, then explained her reasons why.

By the time I was putting TJ back to bed with a full stomach, it was a half hour away from when I'd wake up anyway, so I decided to get an early start on breakfast before I had to be at work by eight that morning.

The entire time, I had a little girl that was very interested in everything I had to say, and a touch of hope that one day we could be more than enemies.

CHAPTER 14

Isn't it weird how we have one hand that knows how to do everything, and one that is useless and can't even open a candy bar?
-Hannah's secret thoughts

Hannah

Two days later, I was in hell.

"I'm sorry, Hannah," the doctor that had hired me all those months ago when I first started, said. "But her father is half of our funding. I'm damned if I do, and damned if I don't."

I stared, dumbfounded.

"I'm fairly certain that it's illegal to fire me," I told him.

He smiled sadly. "Texas is a right to work state. I don't have to have a reason to fire you, honey. I made sure to check with my lawyers on that before I started this."

I was physically sick to my stomach.

"Well, okay," I said, standing up. "I suppose that I will see you around."

He winced. "As of today, you and Travis are no longer welcome at this clinic."

My jaw clenched. "So you're saying that if Travis or I gets sick, that we're not allowed to come here?"

He nodded. "I have a right to refuse service to anyone I deem necessary."

I looked at the ceiling.

"Good to know that you're not banning our kids. Thanks for that at least."

He looked away and gathered his things, actively dismissing me.

I took that as my cue to leave.

I wanted to vomit. Seriously, if there was anything in my stomach, I would have.

God, this was such a nightmare!

How was I supposed to pay my bills? Because I knew one thing, I wouldn't be taking money from Travis. Although, I knew he'd give it to me if I asked.

I'd also have to take TJ out of daycare…

A thought suddenly occurred to me.

A woman that I'd met over a month ago when I'd first come here. A woman that was looking for a caretaker for her mother-in-law. A woman that had looked to be at the end of her wits.

I pulled my keys out of my purse and walked out of the clinic without a single look back, determination in every step I took.

By the time I got to my Jeep, I already had my phone placed to my ear.

Carol Marks was the wife of a local rancher who owned upwards to a thousand acres right outside of town. She was young, maybe twenty-five at most, and was having to deal with the rancher's mother, who was bedridden due to a stroke she'd had six months ago.

The mother, Hilda Marks, was an active rancher with her husband when her husband had died of a heart attack. Two days later, Hilda had a stroke. Ever since then, she'd been bedridden with complete right-side paralysis.

Carol and her husband, Atticus Marks, had brought the mother into the clinic when she'd had her stroke. However, since it'd been so long since she'd had the stroke—which had been in the middle of the night sometime—there was nothing that we could do.

I'd seen Carol quite a few times since then at the grocery store, and other places in town as she did stuff for the ranch and her husband, and each time she'd gotten subsequently more tired.

It had been the day last week when she'd come in for what she suspected as the stomach flu, and was later confirmed as a pregnancy, that she admitted that she'd do absolutely anything for some help. She'd even offered me the role as a caretaker during the daylight hours for quite a large sum of money. Seeing as I had a job, I'd declined.

Now, however…now I was jobless and willing to do just about anything to prove to fucking Allegra that she may have knocked me down, but I was anything but out.

***

An hour later, I was walking out of the Marks homestead with Carol right on my heels.

"If you could just be here on Mondays and Wednesdays, and most likely Fridays from seven forty-five to five in the afternoon, that would make a considerable difference." Carol rubbed her hands together. "Now all I need to do is find someone that can cook."

I snorted. "I unfortunately can't help you there. However, I'd be willing to bet that someone would love to come out here and cook in that kitchen. Thank you so much for everything, Carol. Today has turned into a really good day when it started out to be such a bad one."

She waved my thank you away.

"You have no clue what you're doing for me. I'm so exhausted, and with all this morning sickness going on, I can barely get out of bed most days. God, if it quit, I'd never complain about anything ever again."

I started to laugh. "Says every woman from the beginning of time."

Carol laughed with me.

"I'll also talk to my husband about getting you on the company health plan. Would you be wanting to put the kids on it, too?"

I shook my head. "I'm on Travis' policy. But I appreciate the gesture. Would you like me to come back tomorrow, even though it's Tuesday, and start the regular schedule next week?"

Carol nodded excitedly. "That'll give me time to go to town and get all the errands done that I've been putting off."

Her excitement was contagious, and I found myself amused as I said my goodbyes and drove all the way home.

Since Travis went to pick up the kids, I was left taking my time, and picking up two pizzas for dinner.

The moment I walked in the door, Travis's surprise was evident.

"You're home early…"

I grimaced, my smile long gone.

"Apparently, Allegra and her father are investors in the clinic," I told him.

It took him less than thirty seconds to realize what had happened.

"I'll kill her."

CHAPTER 15

A beard is nature's way of saying let's fuck.
-Fact of Life

Hannah

"Goddammit, I hate this man," Michael muttered, immediately reaching forward and skipping to the next song, but realizing that there was no button to actually skip. "Alexa, skip song!"

I slapped his hand and shoved him away from my counter where my Alexa tower was located.

My brother just laughed.

"Hey, fucker!" I hissed. "I liked that song!"

My brother gave me a droll look.

"You know what I do when I pull someone over and Sam Hunt is playing?" he questioned.

I shrugged, vaguely interested in what he had to say. Honestly, I wasn't sure what he did. It was likely that I wouldn't like it.

"I write them a ticket."

"Right on," Travis muttered as he came into the room, the puppy hot on his heels. "Fucking hate Sam Hunt. Country music poser."

"You know," I smiled, watching the man that had my heart and soul. "You did buy me tickets to see Sam Hunt in concert."

He'd gotten them for me for Mother's Day, and had given them to me last night.

Travis shrugged. "Know you like him."

Michael started to chuckle. "You know that she's going to take you…right?"

Travis looked up at my brother and sneered. "Actually, someone has to stay home with the kids."

That was true…but still.

"My brother can watch the kids…right?" I asked. "Nikki won't care."

Nikki was Michael's wife and I had no doubt in my mind that she wouldn't care.

Nikki started to laugh. "You walked right into that one, big boy."

Michael grunted and turned to his wife. "I don't think I could handle them all by myself."

It was clear that he thought to rope Nikki into helping watch my heathens. Little did he know that TJ had full blown colic, and there hadn't been a night that passed since he was born where I hadn't had to walk with him for hours a night.

"So, tell me about this woman that's ruining your life?"

My brother didn't mince words, and I'd had to give him something to come over here with Travis here.

They were under some sort of truce—a truce that they had to talk about outside for fifteen minutes the moment Michael got here—and so far, it'd been fairly calm.

A lot calmer than it had been the day that I'd given birth, and I woke up to my brother, Travis, my parents, and his parents in the hospital room with me.

Travis and his family were on one side, and my family was on the other.

My baby had been in Travis' arms, and all of them had been sitting so tensely quiet that I'd had the urge to laugh.

Now, though, they chatted amicably about work, the weather, and even about their kids.

I noticed the tension between the two since I knew them both so well, but they were trying…and for that I was grateful.

"She's not ruining…"

"Allegra is a conceited, self-centered, ruthless bitch whose father 'practically owns this county.' Her words, not mine," Travis butted in. "I met her when I was young and dumb, while on leave. We met up another time when I came back on leave, and then I decided while drunk as a skunk that it would be a great idea to get married to her. When I came home for good eight months later, we married, and had a kid within six weeks. What I didn't know, and my whole fuckin' family forgot to tell me, was that she was a catty bitch who thought she was getting somebody that had a lot of money. Unfortunately for her, my father was the one with the money and not me."

My lips thinned.

I hadn't actually heard this story before. I'd wanted to know all about it, but I'd never found the courage to straight up ask Travis why he'd want to go anywhere near Allegra, even with a ten-foot pole.

Hearing that Travis had fallen for Allegra's 'good girl' act had me kind of feeling worried. How did he not see her for what she really was?

But then he explained it better a few moments later, making me think more of him.

"I hadn't spent more than forty-eight hours with her at a time until I got home for good," he continued. "She was like hot and cold. At first, she was hot. She was nice. She was great. Then, after we were married, and she found out that marrying me didn't come with my daddy's money, she started to change. She no longer liked spending time with me. When she was pregnant with Alex, I couldn't get fucking near her. I think we had sex all of four times while I was married to her."

My mouth fell open.

Four times? That was it?

"That's impressive," Michael grunted. "How long were you able to stick it out?"

Travis had a comical look on his face when he answered, "Five years."

I had to laugh at the look of surprise on Michael's face. "You went five years without getting any?"

Travis shrugged. "We were starting up Hail Auto Recovery. When we got that on its feet, we started up Hail House. There wasn't enough time in the day to worry about whether I was getting any."

Michael snorted.

"I should introduce Allegra to Hannah's ex. They seem like they'd be a good fit for each other."

Travis snorted. "As bad as I've heard her ex could be, Allegra would rip off his head and eat his body before he could do more than wave at her."

I giggled and pulled the pot off the stove that I was cooking spaghetti in. I was making Million Dollar Spaghetti—a favorite in this house. The plus side was that it was easy as fuck to make, and that Reggie normally asked for seconds.

That, in and of itself, was a small miracle.

The girl survived on chicken nuggets and sour cream and onion potato chips.

There was literally nothing that kid would eat…but this.

I'd tried it on a whim a few months into my pregnancy because it all sounded so good. I liked cheese. I loved spaghetti. So why wouldn't it all taste good together? Well, it didn't taste good. It tasted divine. So divine, in fact, that I wanted to offer The Pioneer Woman a marriage proposal.

Not that she would ever leave her Marlboro Man for me, but one could hope, right?

Well, that night I tried it out on my daughter, and lo and behold she adored it too. Even asked for second helpings.

Since then, we'd had it at least once a week, and I still wasn't tired of it.

I poured the noodles into the colander and drained them, then set the pot down just as the phone next to my hand rang.

Since it was the house phone, we only had one of them due to us having to have it since we got Internet through the phone company, I wasn't in a rush to answer it. Nobody ever called us on it, so it was a surprise to actually hear the sound.

Nevertheless, I put it to my ear just before it quit ringing and said, "Hello?" All the while I continued to drain the spaghetti.

"Hello, is this the Hail residence?"

I froze at the official sounding voice on the other end.

"This is," I confirmed. "Can I help you?"

The man on the other end of the line didn't beat around the bush.

"I'm the county coroner for Chase County…" he said.

My whole entire being froze.

My parents weren't here in Chase County. They were in Gregg County, which was close. My brother and his family were here, but we were all safe…that only left a few people.

As I racked my brain about who he would be calling about, the man continued speaking.

"I witnessed an accident on the corner of Eighteen Ninety and Meadowbrook," he continued. "A woman and a child…"

My belly soured.

"I'm not calling on official business. The police have already been called, but I just wanted to call you since the woman in the car gave me this number to call."

I was so confused.

"What's her name?"

I was going through all of Travis' brothers.

His mother and father weren't in town. They'd gone to see Tobias and Finley out of state. Reed was deployed. That only left Dante and Baylor.

"Allegra and Alex were in a very bad wreck…"

I looked over to see Travis staring at me, no longer talking.

"What is it?" he mouthed.

I opened my mouth and tried to explain, but the man on the other line was still talking, and I couldn't talk and listen at the same time, apparently.

"The girl wasn't in a restraint. They found her on the side of the road…"

The side of the road.

"The woman was restrained. The police have just arrived," he continued. "My number is…" his voice trailed off as static started to interfere.

"Travis," I mewled. "Alex."

He was in front of me seconds later.

"What happened?"

The line went dead.

"There was an accident."

***

I'd never been so scared in my life.

We made it to the scene in less than ten minutes after Michael and Travis had left, and what I arrived to was utter chaos.

There were emergency crews everywhere.

Two cars were on their sides less than ten feet from each other. Smoke filled the air from both cars. The smell of burnt rubber and something I couldn't decipher were assaulting my nostrils, and the sound of a man yelling as well as a heated engine ticking could be heard over the rest of the noise.

It didn't take me long to locate Travis.

He was being pushed back by a burly police officer on his front side, and Michael on his back. But he wasn't having any of it. He was frantic to get to the other side of what I now realized was Allegra's car.

There were large emergency floodlights erected on all sides of the accident scene, but most of the chaos seemed to be surrounding where Travis was trying to go.

And I knew that was where Alex was.

My heart was literally ripping to shreds.

"This way," I told Baylor.

Baylor was one step ahead of me.

When Travis had left, he'd made me wait for Baylor to get me before I left. It'd been the worst ten minutes of my life.

But now we were there, I could tell that this was very bad.

The moment I got up to Travis' side, I saw the tiny, sequined slip on shoes that I'd bought Alex a few weeks before lying precariously on the edge of the asphalt. One was flipped on its side, and the other was straddling the white line that signaled the end of the pavement.

And just a few feet from those shoes were tiny little feet.

My heart lurched.

"Let me go," Travis shoved at the police officer again. "I'm not kidding, Andi. I need to…"

"You need to back off. You need to let them work. You need to calm yourself down so we can get this done without us having to worry about you instead of her."

That got him calmed down faster than anything else could, knowing that the attention he was garnering from the emergency services crew was actually taking away from them taking care of his little girl.

"All right," he pushed away and immediately placed both hands onto his forehead. "Fuck."

I pushed past Travis, and was stopped by the same cop that had pushed him back. "I'm a nurse," I informed him.

He waved me past him, and I spared one look over my shoulder at Travis before I hurried past and stopped next to one of the medics that was stabilizing Alex for transport.

I tried not to look at her bloodied clothing or the makeshift cast around her arm that clearly indicated she had a broken bone. Nor did I pay attention to the way that her eyes were closed tightly, showing me that she was conscious, but in pain.

The C-spine on her neck, holding her head immobile, was making my hands itch to pull her into my arms and whisper to her that it'd be okay. I wanted to cradle her like the baby she was. I wanted to wipe that blood from her nose and kiss it all better.

But I did none of those things.

"I'm a nurse," I told the medic. "Is there anything I can do?"

He looked at me, and shook his head.

"Life Flight is ten minutes out," he said. "Closest hospital that's not on divert is Children's in Benton, Louisiana."

I nodded, knowing what divert was, and how a lot of the area hospitals were having to go on that due to a high volume of patients lately. When ICU was full, they were practically forced to put the rest of the hospital on lockdown to incoming patients, and the two closest hospitals that were equipped to take a patient in need of the ICU—which was obvious Alex was—had been extremely overwhelmed. Not to mention they were short staffed on top of that.

Children's in Benton was a good choice, if not a little far.

But if that was what had to happen to make sure that Alex had the best care, then that was what we'd do.

And that was what we did.

"Who are you to the little girl?" the medic I'd spoken to minutes before on the side of the road asked as we walked Alex to the waiting helicopter.

"Stepmother," I told him.

It was partially true.

And the moment that I'd come on scene and gotten past the cops that were guarding Alex like a couple of linebackers protecting their quarterback, Travis had seemed to calm even more.

He wasn't happy that they wouldn't let him near her, but having me there was reassuring enough that he stopped trying to push through.

"You're really a nurse?"

I pulled out my badge—the one that was no longer useful since I didn't work at the clinic anymore—out of my pocket, thankful that I'd had the wherewithal to grab it on the way out of the house, and showed it to him.

I thought I'd be using it at the hospital.

"They'll let you ride with her then. They'll always allow medical personnel if the circumstances warrant it," the paramedic explained. "Help me get her onto the gurney."

I did, lifting her slight weight up the foot that it took to get her up on the gurney, and nearly cried out when I heard Alex's low moan.

"Alex?" I murmured, leaning forward, touching the side of her face.

Alex cracked open one eye, and then closed it again.

But it was enough. She knew I was there.

"Can you hear me, honey?"

"Daddy."

The word was so soft, so ragged, that I had to strain to hear it.

But I knew what she was asking.

"He's here, baby," I assured her. "Just a few feet away."

She licked her lip, tried to lift her hand, and then sighed like just doing that one thing had taken it all out of her.

I reached for her hand.

"Are you meeting the helicopter here, or are you transporting her?"

The medic lifted his bags to the bottom of the gurney and fastened them with a few snaps before replying.

"We're meeting them just down the road," he clarified. "There's an open field right next to the library."

I nodded and stood up as the paramedic's partner, a slight woman that didn't look like she was holding her lunch down well, raised the gurney.

I held onto Alex's hand as they walked her to the ambulance.

"How are her vitals?" I questioned.

"Everything was slightly elevated, I gave her some pain meds about a minute and a half before you got there, which is likely the cause of her sleepiness," the medic explained as he helped lift the gurney into the back of the ambulance. "Her arm's broken at least in one place, but likely more since I couldn't set it. Pupils dilated, most likely indicating a concussion. She's got bruises and scrapes, as well as road rash along her left side."

I closed my eyes and stood beside the ambulance for a few moments.

"Once we get her to the LZ—landing zone—and loaded, we'll come back for the mother."

I wanted to say, "Fuck the mother" but managed to hold my tongue.

Instead, I got up into the ambulance, sat down on the bench next to the medic, and bowed my head over Alex's body.

Then I prayed.

I prayed that she'd be okay.

I prayed that she wouldn't have any lasting damage due to this wreck.

I also made a promise to God that I'd make more of an effort to get to know this little girl.

"Ready, Freddy?"

The medic nodded at his partner, and she shut the doors before rounding the ambulance, hopping in the front seat, and driving off.

I looked out the window to see Travis watching, tears coursing down his cheeks, as we sped away toward the LZ.

I held his gaze until I couldn't see him any longer.

***

Travis

I wanted to rewind to yesterday when I last saw Alex, and take her. I wanted to bring her to my house, tell her that she was never leaving again, and that would be the end of it.

But life didn't work like that.

Allegra really had been drinking with my daughter in her care, and then she'd driven.

She had then gotten into a wreck by driving off the side of the road and hitting a parked car.

She'd done a lot of things wrong in this situation. She'd drank with my child under her protection. She'd gotten into the car when she had no business doing so. She hadn't restrained or made sure that Alex had restrained herself. She hadn't seen the parked car due to her inebriated state. Then, she'd wrecked and my daughter had been thrown free of the car.

No father wanted to hear that his kid was hurt.

No father especially didn't want to get a call that not only had she been hurt, but the mother—the woman that you thought you could trust to take care of your baby—had been irresponsible.

"Travis, what are you doing here?"

I tore my eyes away from the retreating ambulance, and turned dead eyes on the woman that was supposed to take care of our baby when I wasn't there to do it.

"Do you know what happened, Allegra?"

I didn't care that she was bleeding from her head, a constant torrent of blood filtering through her hair and down her hairline to curl around her chin.

"I…we got in a wreck." She sounded confused.

That, and she also smelled like a brewery.

"Yes, you did," I confirmed, somehow keeping myself calm. "When did you start drinking?"

I'd half-assed listened to one of the cops trying to get Allegra to talk, but with the state she was in, they didn't know how to handle her.

They were terse with her. Too abrupt, and they didn't sound like they were caring about her state of being, but somebody else's.

I gave her my complete attention, and was acting like she hadn't done anything wrong, when in actuality she'd done a whole lot more than that.

"I didn't," she lied, seeing the trap. "What are you talking about?"

My gaze moved to the officer. "What's her alcohol level?"

"Point two one," he answered. "Almost triple the legal limit."

I turned my attention back to Allegra. "Your daddy won't get you out of this one."

She pursed up her lips and tried to stand, but the officer refused to let her do that.

"Move again and I'll cuff you."

"You can't cuff me!" she declared loudly.

I wanted to yell at her. Scream that she'd fucked up so royally that she'd never see her child again—if our child made it.

However, I held my composure, and looked away. It was one of the hardest things I'd ever done.

I wanted to yell. I wanted to scream. I wanted to tell her she was the worst parent in the world.

The sound of a helicopter brought my attention away from the woman looking like I'd hurt her feelings, and I gazed up to see the Life Flight helicopter coming closer and closer to the ground.

It circled at one point about a half mile away, and slowly started to descend.

I watched, even when it disappeared into the trees.

"Come on, brother." Baylor was suddenly at my side. "They're taking Alex to Children's an hour and a half away."

An hour and a half.

That was going to be the longest drive in the history of drives.

I started to walk to the car, but stopped when something white caught my eye.

A bear.

Alex's bear.

The one I'd bought her years ago that she took everywhere with her. The one thing that had given me hope that maybe she didn't hate me as much as she said she did.

"Travis?"

That was Michael.

He'd fallen in step beside me, but when I stopped, he did, too.

"One second," I said, jogging over to the patch of grass where the bear lay haphazardly.

The moment I had it in my hand, I jogged back to the truck where Baylor was already waiting and slid inside.

Luckily, we were in my actual truck, which had a backseat.

That way, Michael was able to go, too.

Thankfully, Nikki had stayed with the kids.

"Let's go," I ordered. "I want to be there in less than an hour."

Baylor opened his mouth to protest, but Michael beat him to it.

"We'll get there at a respectable time, but if you want to speed, I have a feeling they wouldn't ticket you."

I laughed humorlessly.

"Don't think this day could get any worse."

How wrong I was.

CHAPTER 16

Sometimes I question my sanity, but the voices in my head tell me I'm fine.
-Coffee Cup

Hannah

Riding in the helicopter wasn't anywhere near as bad as I thought it'd be. In all actuality, had the circumstances been different, I would've definitely gotten a lot more out of it—enjoyed it even.

However, I hadn't enjoyed it even a little bit.

Not with Alex moaning every time the helicopter jolted.

She nearly slept through the whole flight, and probably would have the entire flight, but the man in the front seat who was controlling the big bird we were in had a very deep voice like her father's.

Hearing that, Alex had opened her eyes and said, "Daddy?"

My stomach felt like it was tied in knots.

"Just me for now, honey bun." I leaned forward and smiled when Alex's eyes met mine. "You in any pain?"

She shook her head.

That was good. The moment we'd gotten in here, the paramedic and registered nurse, a man in his late twenties or early thirties, had assessed that she needed more meds to make this flight as comfortable as possible.

Wanting her not to be in any pain, I didn't say a word as I watched the man administer the meds, and then monitor her vitals.

Nobody spoke, and I found that I was okay with that. I had a lot of shit swirling around in my brain, and I wanted time to unravel it before we got to the hospital and I had to put the mask back on—the one that reflected cool, calm, and collected.

But staring into Travis' little girl's eyes, the eyes that looked so much like her father, I found it hard to do anything.

"No. Where am I?"

I sat back and pointed to the window. "We're in a helicopter. You were in an accident."

Her brows raised. "Really?"

Her voice was faint, but I could hear what was being said. *Barely.*

"Yeah, sweetheart. Really." I grinned, even though the smile didn't meet my eyes. "Have you ever broken your arm before?"

She shook her head—or tried to—and startled look to find that she couldn't.

"That's a little thing that goes around your neck to keep you from moving it. They want to make sure your neck and head don't have any damage that they can't see. If you move, and you do have something wrong, it could take you longer to heal. And we want you up and running as fast as possible. You have field day coming up!"

The girl smiled, and my heart ripped wide open.

"Will you come to my field day?"

I'd quit my job to make sure that I could make it if I had to.

"Yeah, honey." I smiled. "I think I can do that. Do you want me to bring you lunch?"

She nodded. "But don't forget to bring Reggie something."

I felt tears clog my throat, happy to hear that she didn't want me to forget my daughter.

Progress, if even a little, was a huge stride for us.

"I can do that. We can have a lunch date. Do you like turkey or peanut butter and jelly?"

I knew what she liked, but I wanted to keep her talking. We were very close to the hospital, and I knew they'd want to make sure she was awake and responsive.

"Turkey with white cheese and mustard," she declared.

I grinned. "Your daddy likes the same kinds of sandwiches."

"I like mustard and turkey, too."

I looked up at the pilot, smiling slightly when he entered the conversation.

I wasn't sure how he heard us with all of the noise, but the flight nurse next to me pointed to his microphone that was on his helmet.

I nodded in understanding.

"Who is that?"

Alex tried to look up, but she couldn't look much further than a few inches above her due to the way she was being held down.

"That's Cleo, my brother." The man at my side said to the little girl. "He's got a few kiddos just like you. He's flying really fast, though. He'll beat your daddy to where we're going, but I'm sure he won't be that far behind."

Gratitude coursed through me.

I beamed at him. He looked similar to the pilot, but that was a fleeting thought as Alex caught my attention once again.

"Are TJ and Reggie with you?"

I turned back to the little girl in front of me, and smoothed a few stray hairs out of her face very gently. "No, baby. They're at home with my brother's wife. You remember her, right?"

She nodded. "Your brother's colorful."

I grinned. "Michael is that. He likes his tattoos. Do you like tattoos?"

She smiled. "Daddy has some."

I knew that, too. The one she was most likely thinking of, though, was a single letter on the inside curve of his pectoral, right next to his ribcage. It was the letter A, for Alex.

"Yes, your daddy has some," I confirmed. "Alex," I hesitated. "Do you remember what happened?"

Alex licked the side of her mouth and tasted the blood that was drying on one of the lacerations that marred those cute little puckered lips. "Mommy was mad."

I heard the man at my side growl.

Then the entire helicopter shook.

I gasped and turned, seeing what looked like a bolt of lightning shoot straight down from the sky.

I was in awe.

I'd never, not once in my life, felt like I could reach out and touch a bolt of lightning, but apparently, there was a first for everything.

Alex gasped beside me, and the pilot cursed a blue streak.

Then the almighty thunder started to shake the world around us.

"Goddammit."

I bit my lip and looked back down at Alex. "Did you know that Santa will be here in a little less than seven months?"

Her eyes lit.

Then dimmed.

"What, baby?"

"I'll be with my mommy."

That would be true, *normally*.

However, Allegra had made a very large mistake today by driving with her daughter while she was drunk.

It hadn't escaped me, hearing those words and whispers of those around the accident scene. And the words that the county coroner had spoken to me…well, I'd never forget those. Not ever.

Alex would be with us this Christmas. I didn't care if I had to hire a fucking hitman to take her out. Allegra was through. She. Was. Through.

Not only would Travis make sure that Allegra never saw Alex again, but she was going to learn what a protective mama bear *should* be like.

CHAPTER 17

Keep rolling your eyes, maybe you'll find your brain back there.
-T-shirt

Travis

"You're a fucking madman."

I didn't bother to wait to hear the rest of the argument that my brother and Michael were having.

For once I was happy that my brother, who'd taken defensive driving fifteen times, and lost his license twice, was a fast driver with a lead foot. It got us to the hospital in forty-nine minutes instead of the usual hour and fifteen.

My boots pounded the white tiled floor as I bolted for the reception desk I could see just inside the doors.

In our haste to leave the house earlier, not one of us had taken our phones with us, so there was no way for me to get into contact with Hannah to make sure everything was all right.

Though, I had a feeling that it was bad, but not that bad.

Alex was lucky.

At least that was what I kept telling myself the entire drive to the hospital.

"No running!"

I didn't listen to the old woman behind the desk as I ran up to her.

"My daughter…"

She lifted a single finger. It was obvious that she was used to being obeyed.

I didn't obey anyone, however. I was always a rebel, and right now, I was a rebel who wanted to know how his fucking daughter was…forty-nine minutes ago.

"Young man, you're going to have to go back and walk."

Surely, she was joking.

I was not a child. I was a fucking concerned parent.

"Alex Hail. She's eight. Came here by Life Flight likely about half an hour ago. She was in a car…"

"Young man."

"I've got this," came a terse reply. "Sir, my name is Tru. Your daughter came in a little over twenty-five minutes ago. They've taken her to CAT scan to assess any damage that was dealt to her by her expulsion from the car. She's on the second floor right now. Your wife is with her, in the room. I can take you to where the room is, but you won't be able to enter until they're finished with the tests, okay?"

I nodded mutely.

She led the way, not saying another word.

We took the stairs, thank God, and arrived at the closed door that said, "CAUTION RADIATION" on it.

"Here's where you'll stand. They'll come out in about five to ten minutes. Please, don't get in their way. I don't want to get into trouble with my supervisor for leaving you here, okay?"

I nodded.

She patted me on the shoulder. "I'll just be down here if you need anything. Her room number is room twenty twenty-three. Very back corner, last door on your right, at the end of this hall, okay?"

I looked where she was pointing, and nodded. "Yeah, Got it."

She nodded and left, leaving me to lean against the white wall and look down at the white tiled floor.

There were a lot of things that I'd thought about when my eyes opened today.

One of those thoughts was that I wished Alex were there to see Michael, Nikki, and their kids. They'd seemed to hit it off the last time they were around—even if Michael and I hadn't.

The second thought was that I hoped that Michael didn't kill me for what I'd put Hannah through.

He hadn't done it yet, but I knew the threat was always there.

The third was that I wished Hannah, Alex, Reggie, and our son got along better than they did.

I wanted my entire family together when we were having a family dinner. Everyone was there but Alex, and the bad feeling had continued to grow all damn day long.

I wondered if it was a sense of foreboding. A sense of unease that was crawling down my throat and making my stomach buzz with nerves.

For the next five minutes, I tried to think of anything but murdering my ex-wife, and didn't succeed. I was working on the perfect plan that involved shoving her into traffic when the door opened, and Hannah came out.

"Travis!"

I hugged her to me close, and buried my face into her neck.

"How is she?"

She patted me on the back just as a little voice said, “Daddy?”

I dropped Hannah to her feet, let her go, and moved around her to rush to my little girl’s side.

She was bruised, no longer had the thing on her neck to keep her immobile, and had her arm wrapped to her chest so she couldn’t move it.

Most of the blood was gone, wiped away likely by Hannah, and she was staring at me with wide, fearful eyes.

“Hey, baby.”

She smiled a wobbly smile, and threw her arm up at me.

I took the hint and leaned down, pressing my face against the pillow next to her head.

She wrapped that tiny arm around me, and it felt like she tightened a fist around my heart.

***

Four hours later, I walked out of my daughter’s room, my jaw stiff.

I just spent the last hour holding her down while the nurses started an IV on her. I also held her still while the nurses wrapped her arm in plaster, plain ol’ white because they were out of all the pretty colors.

I listened to her cry and tell the ‘nice policeman’ about what happened with her mom. It wasn’t very clear. From a child’s point of view, who was intimidated by all the people in the room, she wasn’t very informative.

She did happen to say that her mother ‘drank a lot at a party while she sat in an empty room and watched TV.’

That hadn’t been the worst part, though.

Allegra had called me, asking how Alex was.

Apparently, she'd sobered up, and now she was concerned.

Which led me to now, my daughter falling into an exhausted sleep, and me wanting to kill someone.

I found Hannah right outside the door talking to her brother.

The moment she saw me, she turned, and I gathered her into my arms, burying my face back into the side of her neck as I tried to breathe and tell myself that I couldn't take care of my kids if I was in jail.

"She won't be calling you again," Michael promised. "Called a buddy who called a buddy. They took her phone out of her room."

I gritted my teeth and let Hannah go, then blew out a breath.

"You hear all that she said?"

I nodded.

"She also told me on the way to the hospital that her mommy 'always drinks.'" I stretched my neck side to side at Hannah's words.

"I've already contacted our lawyer. He's filing an emergency injunction that'll temporarily give you full custody of her until the rest is settled." She paused. "He thinks that she'll get jail time for this."

I fucking hoped so.

I heard a squeak of shoes, and saw Reggie running toward us.

"Is Alex okay?" she demanded, her little hands on her little hips as she stomped her foot.

I brought her into my side, and she buried her face in my gut as she wrapped her scrawny arms around my waist.

"She'll be okay, honey," I told her.

She let out a relieved breath.

Then I heard the crying.

I looked up to find Nikki heading our way with a very unhappy TJ in her arms.

She looked almost apologetic.

"I tried for an hour," she said. "We drove all the way here with him crying. I know you said he had colic, but damn, girl. This is almost unbearable."

I took my son from her arms, and his tiny frame fit into the crook of my arm with perfect ease.

That didn't stop his screaming, though.

It only ratcheted up a notch.

However, Hannah somehow realized that I needed to hold him, so she let him continue to scream for a good ten minutes before I kissed my boy on his scrunched, pissed off forehead, and handed him to her.

Hannah took him, and he still didn't stop.

In fact, the only thing that got him under control was when she walked to the chair that was just inside the room, lifted her shirt, and latched him onto her breast.

"That'll work for about ten minutes," I told the two people who were staring at me expectantly. "Reggie, girl. Can you go sit in there with Alex? If she wakes up, can you come tell me?"

Reggie nodded enthusiastically, and then she was gone.

I looked back to the two in front of me, and then to the two kiddos behind them that were sitting in the waiting room area just beyond Alex's room. They were both quietly playing on an iPad each, both enthralled and uncaring.

Oh, how the naivety would be nice right about now.

“What are you going to do?” Michael asked.

I looked down at my shoes, raised one hand up above my head, then cleared my throat.

“I’m going to fucking ruin her.”

CHAPTER 18

I'm a real sweetheart, and a real smartass. It's a package deal.
-Hannah's secret thoughts

Hannah

The person that Travis turned into wasn't one I recognized.

He also wasn't the man I fell in love with.

In fact, he was kind of scary, and I wasn't the only one who noticed.

My daughter and Alex had, too.

Alex had come home from the hospital about a week after she'd been admitted.

I'd missed over a week at my job staying there with her. My brother's wife had stayed at our house and kept Reggie in school, while Michael had returned home. Travis had gone back to work, but drove the hour and a half there and back every night to check on Alex.

I kept TJ at the hospital with me, and Alex had gotten quite a bit of bonding time in with her little baby bro.

By the time she was released five days after she arrived, I was sure that someone had transplanted a new kid in Alex…or maybe it was just being away from the venom that her mother spewed at her each and every time her father or I came up.

Regardless, I was enjoying this new little girl, and realizing why her grandmother, grandfather, uncles, and father were so dismayed with what she had turned into over the last year.

And really, I was a hundred percent certain that it all boiled down to Allegra.

Allegra was booked into the county jail, and then bonded out the next day on her own recognizance. Her scheduled court hearing was set for today, and then a little after that, the custody hearing.

Today was a big day, and Travis was acting like a fucking lunatic.

He wasn't saying much of anything, but both the girls, as well as TJ and I, could feel his simmering anger.

He was convinced that today would go bad.

Me? I wasn't sure.

I knew that Allegra's father was the money man in this county. However, the judge that presided over it had proved himself a good man over and over again from what little I'd heard about him.

I was sure that Travis' worries were for naught.

However, I let him fume, and did my normal daily routine of getting the kids up and ready for school and daycare, only with one addition of Alex to the mix.

Everyone was up, clothed, and fed.

They were watching TV quietly when Travis started to angrily slam around the house.

First it was the kitchen cabinets as he tried to find a clean coffee cup.

"They're in the dishwasher," I told him. "I just loaded it and ran it this morning, so you'll either have to open it and wash one, or use your Yeti."

Travis grumbled something under his breath, but went to the cabinet where I kept his Yeti cups—he had twenty of them, no joke.

Once he got his cup, he walked to the coffee maker, and then started to bitch when the cup wouldn't fit underneath the Keurig.

He slammed it down on the counter, and I calmly walked over to him and lifted the drip tray from the Keurig, placed his cup underneath the dispenser, and started it.

He said nothing, but I could practically feel his body shaking with withheld fury.

I walked away without a word and turned to the kids.

"Y'all ready, girls?"

Alex popped up first and walked to the door where her backpack was resting against the backdoor, followed shortly by Reggie.

Reggie shoved her feet into her boots.

"Is Daddy coming to see me today?"

I started to reply to her, saying that her father hadn't communicated with me that he was coming—though he never did. But Travis' reply to her question had me nearly seeing red.

"Your father's a jerk, Reg. He's not going to come, and probably never will."

Reggie's head hung, and Travis, thinking he was helping when he wasn't, ruffled her hair and walked to TJ, gave him a kiss, then walked out of the room.

I walked to where TJ was in his swing, lifted him out, and then walked to the car seat and started buckling him in.

All the while, I counted to twenty in my head so I didn't follow Travis and give him a piece of my mind.

The least the fucker could've done was help me get them in the car…it's not like getting three kids ready to go in the morning was hard or anything. Like getting up an hour and a half early is just the easiest thing to do when you were sleep deprived. But whatever.

Snapping the last of the buckles, I picked up my sleeping baby boy and groaned at the weight of the car seat with TJ in it.

"Getting big, boy," I told him.

Grabbing the bottles of milk from the counter for TJ's meals, I asked Reggie to grab the diaper bag, and we were off.

"Uncle Baylor!" Alex cried out.

She hugged him around the waist, but let him go almost immediately in her rush to get into my Jeep.

Baylor blinked, then focused on me.

"Let me help," Baylor said.

I was surprised to find him right outside the door, but I didn't complain when he took the hulking mass of TJ from my arms and expertly deposited him in the car…like his father could've done.

"Thank you," I sighed, placing the rest of the stuff in the front seat. "What are you doing here?"

"We're riding together to the court hearing."

I nodded. "Oh, okay."

The car seat clicked into the base, and then he backed out of the car, winking at Reggie who was waiting for him to move.

Reggie who still looked very upset.

Dammit.

"Reggie, baby," I whispered. "I'll call your father and ask him if he has plans to come see you today, okay?"

Her face lit up. "Thank you, Mommy."

Then she got into the car, and Baylor gave me a sympathetic look.

He knew the story. He also knew, just like everyone else, how sad Reggie got when he didn't show—which was never.

Yes, she should be used to it by now, but she was a little girl. Little girls wanted their fathers to be in their lives. They didn't understand when their father no longer wanted anything to do with them, or were too busy at work to come down and see them.

After dropping all the kids off at their prospective locations, I drove back home, and used that time to call Joshua.

He didn't answer.

What a surprise.

Sometimes I didn't know why I bothered.

Getting out of the car with a resigned sigh, I walked to the backdoor and barely pushed it open as I bent down to take off my shoes.

That's when I heard Travis.

"I'm never fucking doing it again," I heard him say to Baylor. "It's a pain in the ass, and a fucking joke."

"That's what marriage is about, man. Doing stuff that you don't want to do."

"Well, I don't want to do that, either."

My belly dropped as my throat started to constrict. Tears burned my eyes, and I was on the verge of tears before I'd even walked all the way through the door.

"Hannah?" he asked. "You make sure it was all right with her before you decided this?"

"No. Hannah's awesome, but I'm not doing it again. I'm glad that I didn't do it before because then she'd expect me to follow through."

The words hit me like an anvil straight to the chest.

I swallowed the tears and shut the door a little harder than necessary to announce my arrival home.

Travis and Baylor looked up, and I decided that I needed to tell this asshole Travis, not my usual Travis, that what he was doing wasn't acceptable. Starting with the very first thing he'd done to piss me off this morning.

"I'd appreciate it," I told him, "if you wouldn't intervene when it comes to Reggie's father and Reggie. It's hard enough having to explain to her that he's not coming. I don't need you adding your two cents and breaking her heart."

Travis' face shut down.

"You baby her," Travis countered. "You're not doing her any favors by lying about that piece of shit."

I ground my teeth together and pierced him with a withering glare.

"First of all, you're not her father," I told him. "And apparently, you're not even going to be her *stepfather.*"

Travis' molars audibly snapped together as he tilted his head to the side.

"Yeah, I heard that," I told him. "Would've been nice if you discussed with me that we were no longer engaged, but that's just me I guess."

Travis didn't say anything, and Baylor chose that moment to check out.

He got up without a word and walked outside, leaving both of us alone.

Thankfully.

"Hannah," he stood up.

I clenched my hand into a tight fist and opened my mouth to let him have it, but before I could, a sound came from my purse.

My phone rang, and thinking it was Joshua calling me back, I answered it without looking.

I was pleasantly surprised when I found not Joshua, but Wolf, one of my best friends in the entire world, on the other end.

"Hey, girl."

"Hey, Wolf!" I cried out, happy that he'd called. I could use a dose of happy right now. "What are you doing?"

Wolf and I had met when he was in the hospital recovering from a gunshot wound to his head. I'd been his nurse, and he'd been my patient each shift that I worked until he was released.

Travis also hated him because he was married to his baby sister—and had plans of divorcing her.

Unfortunately, Abby had died in the same accident that had gotten Wolf shot in the head, and Wolf never got the chance to divorce her.

Travis also hated that I was friends with Wolf. He still thought we were more than friends, despite my telling him that we never were more than that.

I knew without looking that Travis' face had turned thunderous.

"I'm in town for something, and just found out about Allegra. What the fuck, Han. Why wouldn't you have told me about that?"

I sighed. "I haven't had time. I'm running behind, and there's absolutely no time to do anything, much less call you and tell you about all the problems I have. And I'm so sleep deprived that any spare moment I have, I use it napping. TJ has colic."

Travis set his cup down and walked out, leaving me alone in the room.

"You don't sound good."

I wasn't.

"I'm okay, Wolf. How's the boy doing?"

Nathan wasn't his son. Nathan was his best friend's son who'd died in the same tragic killings that had taken Abby and almost taken him. Nathan had suffered the same fate as Wolf, but unlike Wolf, he'd not fared as well.

Now, though, he was doing remarkably well for what he'd been put through over the course of his short life. He still had a few developmental delays, but day by day he was smashing every single glass ceiling that was put over him. He was surviving and thriving, and that made me extremely happy.

"He's doing great," he said. "You want to have lunch with me?"

I thought about that. "The hearing is at nine. The custody hearing is at eleven. I can do lunch about twelve thirty if you want."

"That'll work for me. I'll meet you at the courthouse. That's where I'll be anyway."

I didn't bother to ask.

Wolf was working. His cases were almost always confidential. I knew that this was going to be something he couldn't talk about.

"Sounds great."

Then I went about cleaning up after the asshole who couldn't be bothered to put his own fucking cup into the goddamn sink.

All the while, I tried to contain the urge to burst into tears.

CHAPTER 19

If you're waiting for me to give a shit, you might want to get a snack. It's gonna be a while.
-Text from Hannah to Travis

Hannah

I walked out of the courtroom shoulder to shoulder with Wolf, knowing that Travis was behind me, likely staring holes through the back of my neck.

I stopped and turned. "Can you unlock the truck?"

He pulled his keys out and pointed the fob at the truck, which was quite close to the front of the building.

Travis didn't care that he had a large truck and he probably shouldn't park it in a spot reserved for small, compact cars. He never had, and that used to be something that I found endearing in him.

Right then, though, it pissed me off.

Everything about him today was pissing me off.

Fucking asshole.

The moment I got to the passenger side back door, I yanked it open and picked up my concealed carry gun that I'd taken out of my purse in deference to the rules of the courthouse.

Nobody was allowed to carry a concealed weapon into any government building unless they were an officer of the law—on duty.

"You conceal carry?" Wolf asked in complete surprise.

I nodded and put the gun into place in my overly large purse.

"Yeah," I said. "My brother made me get it when I was twenty-one. How did you not know this?"

Wolf shrugged. "That's good thinking. Especially in this day and age."

I nodded and walked with him, stopping in front of his bike.

"You know," I said. "He's really going to kill me if I get on the back of this bike with you."

It was like rubbing salt into an open wound.

I looked over at Travis, who was standing on the side of the walkway next to his truck, staring at me with open anger.

And it wasn't anger at me or at the situation.

Three hours ago, at the first court hearing, Allegra had gotten away with forty-eight hours of community service, and jail time on the weekends from six in the afternoon on Saturday to six in the afternoon on Sunday for the next twenty-eight weeks.

One hour ago, in deference to the new weekend plans that Allegra now had, the judge gave custody over to Travis every weekend, but during the week, she was to be given the choice to stay with her mother if she so wished.

Even I had been flabbergasted, and very angry at that.

Travis, though?

He'd been seconds away from contempt of court. It was only his lawyer who'd kept him in line. His lawyer pretty much said that he needed to get his attitude in check or the judge was going to be problematic.

Then he'd looked at me so angrily as if it'd been all my fault, and I'd sat back in my chair and blinked.

Blinked.

I'd never, not once, had that much anger directed at me.

That was until Allegra had looked over at me seconds before she was led out of the courtroom for her new weekend plans.

The look she gave me would've flayed skin off of a lesser woman's bones. Naturally, I'd folded my arms across my chest and stared at her just as angrily back, and something had slid through her gaze. A promise of retribution.

Luckily, I was made of hardier stuff, and controlled my anger—unlike Travis—and waited until she was led out of the courtroom before standing up and leaving.

That had led me to now, as I sped walked toward Wolf's bike, with a very angry Travis at my back.

"Your husband-to-be isn't going to kill you," he promised.

The sick feeling in my stomach only got bigger.

"He's not my husband-to-be," I managed to tell him.

Then, with a new pep in my step, I got on the back of Wolf's bike—like I'd done quite a few times before—and waited for him to mount in front of me.

He did, but I didn't scoot closer like I would've once done.

No matter how pissed off I was at Travis, Wolf had a wife now. A wife that I adored, and I'd never do that to.

I attempted a look under my lashes out of the side of my eye at where Travis had last been standing and nearly jolted at the look of cold fury in his eyes.

Oh, yeah. He was pissed. So pissed, in fact, that I knew I'd hear it when we got back.

Did that stop me from leaving? *No.*

Did that stop me from laughing when Wolf said something to make me giggle moments later? *No.*

Why? *Because Travis was a big, fat jerk.*

CHAPTER 20

Mom: Watch your language.
Me: Oh, fuck. Sorry.

Travis

"You're being a complete dick to her," Baylor pointed out.

I flipped him off and walked to the truck that I'd unlocked for her.

"What'd she get out of here?" Baylor asked curiously.

"Her purse?" I guessed.

"No, she had her purse with her," he said.

I thought about that for a moment. I didn't know what she got if it wasn't that. Maybe her water bottle? She'd been trying to drink more water lately.

I shrugged. "Then I don't know. Not that I really care, either."

He grumbled something under his breath that I didn't bother asking him to clarify. I didn't really want to know what my brother thought. What little he'd told me already this morning was enough for me to know that I didn't want to hear any more.

He thought I was being an ass, and maybe I was.

But all in all, I was just pissed off.

I fucking hated the system and how things worked. I hated that Allegra was able to get the hell out of jail on her own fucking recognizance only hours after she'd had an accident that had put our daughter in a Life Flight helicopter hours away. I hated that she came up to the hospital acting like a concerned mother only a day later.

And the icing on the cake was what the judge had just done.

Who the fuck would give a woman that had almost killed her own daughter fucking jail time on the weekends so it didn't fuck with her work? Work that she did with her own father, so they couldn't even say she'd be fired due to missing.

Yeah, I wasn't buying it.

Her father had done something.

Then, he'd then given Alex the choice to go home with her during the week while she wasn't in jail—and we all knew how that would turn out. Alex would go, and then I'd get her back, and she'd be the same hateful kid that she'd been before her accident.

So no, I wasn't mad. I was angry. I was furious. I was livid.

I was sad.

Then, after all of that had gone down, I'd walked out of the courthouse, intending to apologize to Hannah, only for her to ride out on the back of some other man's bike. The same man that had been about to divorce my baby sister before she was killed.

Which meant now I was angry with her, too.

"I feel like it's deserved, don't you think?" Baylor asked.

I looked over to him and walked around the back of the truck, trying not to watch as Wolf and Hannah rode out of the parking lot.

"I think that she got a sentence," he said. "It may not be what we were looking for, but I'm guessing it's about as good as we could expect."

I opened the truck and got inside, looking over at him.

"How do you figure?" I snapped. "I was hoping for her to be in there for at least two fuckin' years."

The lawyer said since Allegra had been charged with a DWI—driving while intoxicated—with a child passenger under the age of fifteen, that she could face up to two years in prison. And that was before all the assault charges were placed on her due to what Alex had faced after the wreck.

"She's the county favorite," Baylor replied. "Everybody knows her. Her father kisses everyone's asses so he can schmooze them. Hell, just last month, he gave the judge a really good deal on a car."

I started the truck and backed out of the spot, then accelerated a little too fast as I made my way home.

"Anyway, I guess what I'm saying is that you're lucky she got anything," he continued, not noticing my shitty driving because he drove even shittier. "Plus, from the way Alex has spoken over the last few days, I don't really see her voluntarily going back to her mother."

I frowned and looked toward him momentarily to gauge what he was saying.

"What do you mean?"

"I mean that over the last couple of days, she's asked everybody and their brother if she has to go back to her mom's, and when we say 'no' she looks all relieved and shit."

I thought about that for a moment.

She'd asked that when we got her home from the hospital a few days ago, and then again this morning before she returned to school. When I'd told her that she wouldn't be going back for a while, she'd looked relieved. In fact, she'd hugged me so hard that I worried about the state of her fractured ribs.

But she'd hugged me, and then had skipped away.

"I guess I can see that," I murmured under my breath. "But it won't be long before she's asking to go back. I know she misses her."

"See, that's where you're wrong, too."

I pulled onto the road that led to the school, and then past it to our house, and swung into the school's lot instead.

I needed a fuckin' hug, and I wouldn't be getting one from Hannah. My daughter was going to have to hug me instead.

I sure as fuck didn't want one from Baylor.

"Why do you say that?" I put the truck into park once I pulled into a spot.

"I think that she doesn't want to go back," he answered. "I happened to overhear her and Hannah talking, and she asked if she was going to get her own room now."

Right now she shared a room with Reggie when she came over. We didn't have enough rooms for them all to have their own room, and since at the time Alex hadn't lived with us, I hadn't seen a reason to buy a house with the extra bedroom.

But if she was staying with me permanently, then I'd definitely start looking for somewhere else to stay.

"Be back," I muttered.

CHAPTER 21

Boyfriend & boy friend. That space is the friend zone.
-Fact of Life

Hannah

I waved at Wolf as he dropped me off beside my car and said, "I'll see you in a couple weeks. What does Nathan want for his birthday?"

Wolf shrugged his large shoulders. "Baseball stuff…Star Wars shit. I don't know."

I rolled my eyes and waved at him one more time. "Go. Let me know when you get home okay."

He gave me a thumb up.

"Oh, and tell Raven to make sure she gives me an idea of what I need to bring."

He gave me an 'okay' sign with his thumb and forefinger, then gunned his motorcycle and drove away.

Before I could get into the house, though, my phone rang.

I looked at the caller ID, which said it was the daycare.

"Hello?"

"Umm, Hannah, are you okay?"

I frowned. "I am, why, what's wrong? Did Travis forget to get something?"

TJ's daycare teacher snorted. "You could say that. Was he supposed to be getting TJ today?"

My stomach sank.

I looked at my watch and saw I was running late.

"Yes," I moaned. "He didn't, did he?"

"No," Angel said. "And Reggie's here, too."

I frowned. "Alex?"

"No, not Alex. She didn't get off with Reggie. Reggie said that Travis picked her up."

I clenched my back teeth together and angrily yanked open my car door. "I'll be there in five minutes, tops."

I didn't wait for her to hang up as I backed out of the driveway, going a little too fast.

My tires squealed in protest as I slammed on the brakes and accelerated down the road at a speed probably not meant for a neighborhood.

Regardless, I drove at least ten over the speed limit the entire way to the daycare and arrived within eight minutes, not ten.

My kids were the only ones left in the entire building, and I started apologizing the moment I pulled the front door open.

"I'm so, so, so, so sorry," I apologized. "I didn't know that Travis didn't get them."

She waved the apology away.

"I know. And it's truly not a big deal. However, since you're late, the daycare owner won't let me get away with not charging you the late fee. It's two dollars a minute."

I looked at the clock. It was six thirty-three. That was sixty-six dollars that I didn't have. I pulled open my purse and unzipped the secret compartment that I used to hold my extra petty cash for a rainy day. After counting off sixty-six dollars, I handed it to her and shoved the last five that I had back into the pocket.

"I'm so sorry," I repeated. "I know you say it wasn't a big deal, but I still feel like shit."

She smiled gently at me. "No big deal, honey. Everyone does it."

Not me, I wanted to say. Instead, I just smiled. "Thank you again. I'll see you tomorrow."

Reggie reached for TJ's diaper bag as I reached for TJ, who was strapped into his car seat, asleep.

Asleep.

I winced.

That would mean that he'd be wide-awake here in the next few minutes or so, and that would also mean that he'd be late going to bed. Which would make *me* late going to bed.

Wonderful.

"What happened, Mom?" Reggie asked as she walked at my side out to my Jeep.

I swallowed the words that threatened to come out and controlled my emotions before saying, "I don't know, honey. I'll figure it out, though."

That was for damn sure.

Travis was also supposed to make dinner. My guess was that he forgot to do that, too.

Hence the reason for swinging into McDonald's and ordering two Happy Meals for the girls before driving home.

By the time I pulled back into the driveway, TJ was well and truly pissed off and very much awake, and I was on the verge of tears.

After the day I'd had, I was convinced the day couldn't get any worse.

I was wrong.

CHAPTER 22

Some things in life are better left unsaid. Which I generally realize after I've said them.
-Face of Life

Travis

"I'm hungry, Daddy."

I looked up from the motor I was tinkering with and let my eyes move to the clock.

Then my stomach dropped.

Six forty-nine pm.

Holy fuck.

I dropped the wrench I was using to tighten a bolt and reached for Alex's hand. "Come on, we have to go get…"

The door of the garage was kicked open, and Reggie came barreling inside, two Happy Meals in her hands. "I got food!"

Alex semi-clapped her hands together due to the cast on her arm and reached for the meal that Reggie was holding out to her.

Together they turned on their heels and walked back inside, and I followed at a much more sedate pace.

I could hear TJ hollering his displeasure the moment I rounded the corner of the kitchen, and I winced when I saw Hannah standing at the sink staring down at the dirty dishes…dishes I was also supposed to do.

TJ was in the seat on the counter directly next to the sink, and she started muttering under her breath when she turned on the faucet.

When she reached for the first pot, I stopped her by saying, "I'll do that."

She turned only her head and glared. "If you were going to do them, I'd think you'd have already done them."

I didn't have much to say to that.

She was partially right and partially wrong. I'd forgotten, yes. But that didn't mean that I wasn't going to do them at all. Eventually, I would've come into the kitchen and seen them there filling up the sink, and then I would've washed them. Sure, it might be after dinner…oh, shit.

Not only had I forgotten to pick the kids up from daycare, but I'd also forgotten to cook dinner. Oh, and let's not forget to wash the goddamn dishes.

I barely restrained myself from slapping my forehead in complete and utter failure.

"Hannah," I started.

She shook her head. "I'm not in a good place right now. Please don't make me start yelling at you in front of the kids."

I snapped my mouth shut and then walked over to where she was standing.

I'd had a bad day.

I'd had a really, really bad day.

I'd started it out bad by Hannah walking in and overhearing what I was saying to Baylor—which had been me talking out of my ass, doing something stupid.

Then, I'd had to deal with all that shit swirling around me due to what Allegra had done.

The icing on the cake had been arriving outside once it was all over and seeing Hannah get on the back of a man's bike—a man that I had a lot of unfinished business with.

Then I'd gotten my girl so I could have a talk with her about her mother, and what had gone down that day. And she'd calmed me down by saying just a few short words— 'I want to stay with you, Daddy. I don't want to go with her.'

And that had been the last of my anger.

So we'd talked, and caught up, and I hadn't thought much about the rest of the afternoon. I hadn't thought about dinner or getting the kids from daycare.

I hadn't thought much of anything but spending time with a kid that didn't tell me she hated me every chance she got anymore.

And I could tell without even speaking to her that Hannah was pissed.

Honestly, I couldn't say that I blamed her.

"Okay," I said, knowing when to stop. I was by no means finished with this conversation, but I knew that it needed to happen without the kids aware of every single thing that came out of our mouths.

So instead, I picked my son up and cradled his angry body to my chest.

He only wailed louder.

This, although kind of sucky, I could handle.

I could handle angry babies.

I could handle angry kids.

I could not handle Hannah's anger. It hurt.

It physically hurt my heart to think of her upset in any way, and I knew that I was the one to make her upset. I was the one that put that frown on her face. I was the one that said something this morning that I didn't mean.

Yeah, I had a lot of shit to make up for.

And I'd do that starting now.

Stopping next to TJ's diaper bag, I pulled out the pacifier and popped it into his mouth.

It wouldn't stop him from crying for long, but until he figured out that he didn't like it, the screaming would be at an end.

"Travis, you forgot us."

I winced at Reggie's accusing words.

"I'm sorry, girl," I told her sincerely. "I didn't mean to forget you. I was working out in the garage, and since there were no windows, I couldn't see that the sun was setting—signaling it was time to come get you. I'm sorry, Reg. Forgive me?"

Which was the truth. The garage had no windows, and if the garage door wasn't up, then I had no basis for what time of day it was unless I looked at the clock on the wall. And even then, it was hit or miss on whether or not that was the real time or not.

That wasn't a good enough excuse, though, and we both knew it.

"If you got me a phone, I could've called you and told you it was time to go," she pointed out.

I grinned at her. "I think you mentioned needing a phone, but tell me, does an eight-year-old really need a phone?"

She nodded enthusiastically, as did my daughter.

"We really do."

I rolled my eyes and looked down at TJ, who was sucking on his paci without a word of protest. The champ.

I sighed. "I'll think about it."

Reggie grinned. "In that case, yes, I forgive you."

I wish it was going to be that easy to deal with her mother.

A mother who was staring at me over her shoulder like I'd just promised her daughter a one-way trip straight to hell.

Shit.

Deeper and deeper I went.

Her eyes fell to TJ who was happily chilling in my arms and then back to my face before she turned around and started washing the dishes again.

"You want some bacon and eggs?" I asked her.

That I could make fast, and I knew that she liked them.

Hannah shrugged.

"I managed to go get Bear's Smokehouse bacon on the way home…"

Hannah's shoulders slumped slightly.

"And I got buttermilk. I can make pancakes," I continued.

Hannah sighed.

Still she didn't speak.

So that was either one of two things. Yes or no.

I decided to go with yes and went about getting the electric skillet out and plugging it in before I got the bacon out.

I shifted TJ up to my shoulder and bounced him lightly as I used one hand to open the bacon and start setting it out on the quickly heating surface.

The bacon sizzled, filling the room with noise, as Reggie and Alex continued to talk about the benefits of having a phone as an eight-year-old.

They were on number seven, which was being able to call me or Hannah anytime they wanted—and yes this was number seven instead of number one—when Hannah shut off the sink, signaling the end of the dishes.

"You all right with him for a little while?"

I nodded, but needn't have bothered. She was already walking out of the room by the time my head started to nod an affirmative.

"Can I have some bacon?"

I looked over to see both girls staring at me.

"Didn't y'all just eat?" I queried, eyeing their trash.

Reggie nodded. "We did, but we're still hungry."

Of course, they were.

I added six more pieces of bacon to the skillet before transferring TJ over to the other arm.

He was heavy for two months old, but I guess that was my fault, too.

I was a big kid growing up, and it was more likely than not that TJ would be, too.

The paci came out of TJ's mouth when I moved him, causing him to start winding up for a good scream. Luckily, I was able to bend down, pick it up, and pop it back into his mouth.

“Mommy doesn’t like when I give that to him when it hit the floor,” Reggie pointed out.

“What Mommy doesn’t know won’t hurt her,” I told her.

“I heard that.”

I winced and looked over my shoulder to see Hannah striding into the room.

She was now dressed in loose wide-legged pants, a gray ribbed tank top, and white socks.

She wasn’t wearing a bra, and I instantly felt my reaction to her in the way my jeans fit.

“Over easy or scrambled?” I asked her.

She didn’t answer. What she did do was take TJ out of my arms, and then go sit in the recliner on the other side of the counter in the living room, and pulled her shirt down to expose her breast.

I gritted my teeth and closed my eyes, counting to ten.

Yeah, I’d fucked up. She was pissed. It didn’t take a genius to figure that out.

Fuck.

The silent treatment was answer enough.

Dinner went like this.

The girls spoke.

They ate my bacon.

Hannah ate her food in the living room—as far away from me as she could get.

I washed up, put the dishes in the dishwasher, and cleaned up my mess.

All the while she said not one single word to me.

Alex and Reggie chattered like nothing was wrong, and I guess, in their little world, that there wasn't anything wrong. Which meant I was doing my job correctly as a parent, and so was Hannah.

That was something that Allegra never really got in control of.

If she was pissed, everyone within a square mile of her would fucking know it.

It was like a breath of fresh air not having Hannah light into me with the kids around.

"Daddy, can we get into your shower?"

I looked over at Hannah, who had her back to me.

She subtly nodded, and I looked back toward Alex.

"Yes, y'all can," I said. "But make sure you hang your towels up, and if I find all those Barbie dolls in the shower again, you won't take another one in there again, got it?"

Both girls nodded eagerly and ran toward Hannah's bedroom.

"You want anything to drink?"

She shook her head no.

Goddammit.

"Daddy, I can't get it hot!"

I sighed and made my way to the bathroom, turned it 'hot' for them, and sat down on the bed and waited for them to finish.

They did, twenty minutes later, and I still was no closer to figuring out what to do or say to Hannah than I had been when I walked to their room and sat down on Reggie's bed to wait for them.

When they came in fully dressed, I pointed to their beds.

They hopped in them and situated themselves, but continued to carry on as if it were midday instead of nearing two hours past their bedtime.

"G'night, girls," I drawled to the two giggling hyenas. "Don't make me come in here and turn this TV off because y'all are talking, okay?"

Both girls nodded enthusiastically, and I gave them each a kiss before leaving the room.

When I came out from saying goodnight to them, Hannah was just coming out of TJ's room.

We both stilled in the hallway, staring at each other.

She much more warily than I was.

"Wanna take this to our room?"

She didn't say anything but headed in the direction of the bedroom. The moment we both crossed the threshold, I closed the door and locked it for good measure before turning around to study her.

She was sitting in a chair that usually had clothes in it in the corner of the room.

I didn't know where to begin. There was so much that I needed to apologize for, that I went with my gut.

"I don't understand why me not celebrating Valentine's Day is a cause for you to go off on me," I blurted.

I mean, nobody could ever say that I wasn't good at words. Right?

She tilted her head.

"I don't know what you're talking about." She crossed her arms angrily over her chest. "I went off on you today because you made Reggie cry."

My heart thudded against my rib cage.

"I never meant to make her cry, Han," I told her. "But Joshua isn't going to be a part of her life. I've been in her life for a year now, and not once have I seen him. If he were going to be around, he'd be here by now. I would've seen him." I hesitated in what I had to say next, knowing that it wasn't going to be nice to hear. "You're doing her a disservice by not telling her that he's a piece of shit."

"I can't tell my daughter that her father is a piece of shit," she shot back.

I waved my hand in the air to clear it. "That's not what I mean, and you know it. You need to stop telling her you'll call. You need to tell her that it's a possibility that he's not going to come, and stop giving her false hope that today will be the day that he actually shows."

She looked away.

I knew that I'd hit home with that one.

"In the year or so that I've been in her life, I've watched her cry over the fact that he's not around, and it fucking hurts to see. I know it does. The problem is that I'm a better father than he ever has been, or will be."

"Yeah, right," she snorted. "You forgot my kids today. I noticed how you didn't forget yours."

I clenched and unclenched my jaw.

"I'm sorry," I said. "I never, not ever, would've forgotten Reggie or TJ on purpose. I was in the garage, I'd left my phone in the house, and I had to take my watch off to work on the pistons in the motor," I told her. "I'm not used to picking them up, Han."

She shot me a glare.

"Well, that's the truth."

My stomach tightened. "What's that supposed to mean?"

"It means that you don't have anything to do with picking them up. I have to pay for the daycare. I'm the one that lost my job because of your ex-wife. I'm the one that had to scramble to find something, and take it even though I really didn't want to do that job."

"Every time I give you money for the daycare bill, you leave it on the counter."

She looked away.

"Why?"

She took a deep breath, and then let it out.

"Joshua tried to control our marriage with money," she said, finally giving me her eyes for the first time since this discussion started. "It started out with help with nursing school, then morphed into him paying for Reggie's daycare, my car note, the house note. It all spiraled, and when he left, I was financially dependent on him for everything. It nearly broke me."

I fucking hated Joshua. He was a jerk and a half. As if I didn't hate him enough for what he'd done to Reggie each time that she waited outside for a man that was never going to show up, now I had to hear this.

"TJ is half my child, Han," I told her gently. "And my mother would love to watch them for free. Which she offered to you from the beginning." I held my hand up when she went to argue with me. "And I know that you don't want to put her out, but my mother would absolutely adore watching him."

She blew out a breath.

"She can watch him."

"As for what Allegra did, I can't change that now. I've already spoken with my lawyer on the matter. He says that in all actuality, the clinic didn't need to give you any explanation to why they fired you at all. I know that it was Allegra. You know that it was Allegra. And honestly, I know that the family you told that you'd work for is nice, but that's not your passion. You could've just as easily applied at the hospital the next town over. You could also work for me, but I didn't want to offer that and you think that I'm offering my fiancée a handout when it's just the opposite. I need someone there that I can trust. Someone that can take care of all the shit that I don't have time for. Stuff that Dante used to take care of before he left."

That's when tears hit her eyes.

"Fiancée?" She laughed even as tears started to stream down her cheeks. "That's rich after what I heard today."

I frowned. "That's the second time you've mentioned that now. What exactly do you think you heard?"

"I'm not doing it again. I'm glad that I didn't do it because then she'd probably expect it," she said with so much derision that it nearly gutted me.

I frowned as I thought back to what I'd said earlier.

"If you didn't want to marry me, you should've just told me. I would've understood. It would've hurt, but not anywhere near as much as hearing you say that to your brother when you thought I was gone."

That's when I finally understood. She'd overheard my conversation earlier about Valentine's Day and had then thought that I was talking about not marrying her. That I wouldn't do it again.

I got up and crossed the room in half a second, and was leaning over her chair, my fists on either side of her, as I bent over and gave her my eyes. My angry eyes.

"I'm going to tell you this once, and once only." I leaned further forward until our faces were only inches apart. "I *am* marrying you. I don’t care what Allegra says. I don’t care what you say. I don’t care what the fuckin’ Pope says. You. Are. Mine.”

CHAPTER 23

Who cares if girls look different without makeup? Your dick looks different soft.
-Text from Hannah to Travis

Hannah

"You. Are. Mine."

Those words were like a balm to my broken soul.

My heart was thundering in my chest, and I was staring at the man that made my belly flutter with nerves, as I tried to find something to say to that three-word statement.

Three words that changed my entire demeanor.

If Joshua had said that when we were together, I would've told him that I wasn't anybody's—not even his. If somebody asked me that same question right now, I would have no problem saying that I was Travis'.

I really was his.

I was his, and nobody else's.

Even as pissed as I'd been at him, I'd never once considered leaving him.

Now, when he was pissed and in my face, with his beard tickling my chin, I realized two things.

One, I'd never leave him. He could be scary Travis all he wanted, and I'd never leave. Which was scary in and of itself.

Number two? The man really got my motor revving.

I'd felt like shit all day. I was fairly sure my period would begin any second, and I'd gone most of the day thinking that my man didn't want to marry me after all.

I'd changed into the shittiest pajamas that I could find thinking Travis wouldn't get anywhere near me in them.

I was wrong.

He got near me.

He was in my face. His mouth was inches from mine. And he was *angry.*

So angry, in fact, that I knew that I might've pushed him just a little too far.

"I've never, not once in my life, had something as good as you."

Those words. God. They really hit home.

I'd never been someone's best. I'd always been second. Third. Last.

"I've said I love you to you," he said. "But I've never told you why."

"Why?" I squeaked.

"Yeah, why," he confirmed.

I licked my lips, and if he'd just been a little bit closer, I might've gotten his, too.

"Okay," I whispered.

"You ready?"

I nodded.

"First Abby died."

My heart stuttered in my chest.

His first sister, Abby. She'd passed almost four years ago now.

"My second sister, Amy."

I closed my eyes as his pain washed over me.

"Dante's family."

Tears choked my throat.

"Allegra pulling her bullshit."

I opened my eyes.

"If you hadn't been there with me through all of that, to listen to me bitch. God," he shook his head and took a deep breath, "I can't tell you what it did to me to hear my little girl tell me she hated me. Over. And over. And over again."

I lifted my hand up and touched his face.

"God, it hurt so bad." His voice cracked. "But you were there to talk me down. You were there to tell me that it was all going to be okay. You were there when I needed someone to talk to when my own family was too broken to listen."

I was.

"I'd listen to you talk about just about anything," I whispered. *"Anything."*

His smile was heartbreaking.

"You, with your pretty blonde curls and your soft-spoken voice…you were there when I needed you the most. But that's not the only reason why I love you," he whispered. "I love you because you're willing to do anything for my girl. I love you because you brought my son into this world. I love you even though you almost died doing it. Your stupid stubborn pride. I love you because when I hear your voice, I know that today is going to be a good day, no matter what happens beginning, middle, or end."

Tears were now actively leaking out of my eyes.

"You're good with words," I said hoarsely. "I was ready to throw down with you. Now I don't know whether to kiss you or rip your clothes off."

His grin was wicked. "Do I get a choice in what you choose?"

I nodded. "Absolutely."

He lowered his mouth to mine and pressed those beautiful, soft lips against my tear-stained ones.

"Then I choose both."

Then I was up and out of the chair, lifted by both of his large hands on my hips.

I went with him, wrapping my hands around his neck as I continued kissing him. Even with him slowly pushing my pants down my hips.

He didn't stop and question me about my granny panties. Didn't stop to do much of anything but break the kiss when he lifted the shirt up and over my head.

But he was back, even hungrier than before the moment that I was standing bare in front of him.

"You're so beautiful," he whispered against my lips, skimming his way down the length of my jaw. Then further down to the shell of my ear.

His hands smoothed down my naked sides, fingernails dragging deliciously against my curves.

I didn't feel beautiful. In fact, I was sure that he'd not had a good chance to actually look at the underwear he'd pulled off of me.

They were my 'I'm expecting my period' panties. The ones that you put on that you don't care about. The ones that are stained and ripped.

I was fairly positive that they had a hole somewhere near my left ass cheek.

That was the way it was with Travis, though. He didn't care about what I wore, or that I had stretch marks. He didn't care that some days I was a bitchy person. He loved me for me, and I was doing him a disservice by not loving him for him.

And I would change that. Right fucking now.

My hands on his abs, I moved my hands down to skirt underneath the tail of his shirt, and then pushed up.

He got the hint and raised his arms high above his head, grinning wickedly when I was only able to get it up to his elbows.

"Help me," I ordered softly, my eyes hooded with barely contained passion.

He did by bending at the waist and allowing me to pull the t-shirt the rest of the way off him.

He stood and started unbuckling his own belt and pants, then pushed them down to his ankles.

That's when I realized that sometime between him lifting me from the chair, and taking my clothes off, he'd discarded his boots.

Oh, and let's not forget that he wasn't wearing underwear.

That I realized right off the bat when he stood up, and his erection nudged me on the hip.

"You don't have any underwear on." I pointed out the obvious.

He grinned and dropped to his knees.

"No, I sure the hell don't."

I licked my lips.

"Why?"

He lazily stroked his hand over my belly and then down to my thighs.

"There was this woman who came in the house really mad earlier, and instead of asking her where my underwear was that she washed, I chose to freeball it instead so she didn't release the dragon on me."

I laughed, throwing my head back, and belting one out.

Then I felt the bite of his teeth on my belly, and I grinned down at him.

"They're in your drawer…where they belong."

He rolled his eyes. "Of course, they are."

I sifted my fingers through his hair, letting my nails drag along the base of his scalp the way he liked.

He growled like a content cat and nuzzled my belly.

The move made my pussy clench.

He was so close, yet so far away.

"Travis."

That one word, leaving my lips like it did, was enough for him to laugh like the ass he was.

"You're not nice," I whimpered.

His eyes changed, becoming hot.

"Turn around."

I bit my lip and slowly turned in his arms, shivering slightly when his mouth came into contact with my ass cheek.

"Bend over the chair," he breathed, biting my ass.

Chills danced down my spine as I did what he ordered, placing my elbows on the arm of the chair and turning my head to look at him.

"Eyes down," he ordered. "I don't want you prepared for what I'm about to do to you."

I bit my lip and returned my gaze back forward, staring at the seat of the chair as I thought about what he was about to do to me.

He didn't want me to prepare?

What was he going to do that he didn't want me to brace myself for?

Then I felt his tongue, wet and hot, on the seam of my pussy lips.

I moaned and dropped my head even further to rest on the cool leather covering the arm of the chair.

My legs were already shaking with anticipation.

For the longest second, I swear he just stared at what was before him. He studied it, pinching first one pussy lip, and then the other.

Then came the lick again, this time his tongue diving between those lips and sinking into the most intimate part of me.

He didn't linger for long, though.

A quick swipe. A tease, and then he was gone.

"Fuck," I breathed out shakily.

Then he blew a breath against my overheated core, and I swear to God, I almost climaxed right then and there just by the tiniest bit of attention that his breath gave my body.

I inhaled sharply, squeezing my eyes shut tight, as I tried to tell myself how embarrassing it would be if I came within seconds of him *blowing on me.*

"Han?" he breathed, bringing his palms up the outside of my thighs. "It's okay to come."

"I don't want to yet," I keened. "I want to come so hard and long that I forget how to breathe. I want to have you inside me when I do. What I don't want is to embarrass myself by coming like a four-pump chump."

He started to chuckle.

And when I was least expecting it, he trailed his tongue to my back entrance.

I squeaked and tried to stand up, but his sudden grip on my hair had me halting before I could even straighten.

"Stay," he growled, sounding completely unwavering in his order.

I froze.

"I-I've never d-done that."

I felt his beard on the outside of my thigh as he kissed the back of my thigh.

"No, you haven't," he agreed. "But you're about to."

Before I could deny him, he was back, this time with a wet finger circling that forbidden entrance.

"Travis," I whispered. "Are you sure that…"

That's when the sharp crack of his hand came down so hard on my ass that I squealed.

"No screaming or you'll wake the baby, and then I'll have to get creative."

I growled.

That would not be happening. Our kid slept like a rock, once he finally went to sleep—just like his father.

I did manage to keep my screams in my throat, however, as he pressed his finger insistently to my back entrance.

This time he brought his other hand up and trailed it along the length of my sex, dragging his fingers along the distended little bundle of nerves.

"I'll try," I promised. "But swear to God, Trav. I'm not sure I can keep being quiet if you go any fur…"

He pushed that finger further, and the words I was saying became stuck in my throat.

Never, not once, had I thought that having his finger inside my ass would be erotic.

However, Travis lived to prove me wrong, and prove me wrong he did.

It was not only erotic, but it was amazing.

The stretch and burn of his finger filling my ass was only the very beginning.

The tip, as one would say.

I swallowed and told my galloping heart to take a break, but then he sucked my clit into his mouth, momentarily distracting me from the feeling of my ass stretching around his finger.

Just when I was on the verge of crying out, knowing that I wouldn't be able to hold it in much longer, he replaced his pinky finger with something bigger.

His thumb, which was coated in the juices that were practically leaking out of me at this point.

I buried my face into the crook of my elbow and groaned.

"Yes, yes," I rocked my hips.

I had no control of my body anymore.

Everything that I did was something that *he* was making me do.

And when I lifted one leg and placed it on the chair next to my elbow, giving him easier access, that was enough to send me to my tip-toes.

"Fuck," I whispered. "Trav."

He squeezed my clit between two fingers and flattened the palm of the hand that belonged to the thumb in my ass against my spine.

My eyes were squeezed so tightly shut that I wasn't sure if it was light or dark in the room anymore. I was seeing stars, and with a wiggle of his thumb, I lost the battle with my orgasm.

One second I was hanging on by a few spare threads, and the next I was soaring so high that the scream left my throat whether I wanted it to or not.

I came so hard that I didn't even feel him stand up behind me. Didn't feel the tip of his cock sitting at the entrance to my pussy.

Didn't feel him slide inside until the swing of his balls hit my over-sensitized clit.

I bit down on my arm, moaning despite his telling me not to.

I no longer had control of anything. Not a single thing.

Not the way I would cry out each time he slammed inside of me. Not the way the chair rocked with our unsteady weight. Not the way I was biting down on my skin, digging deep indentations that were on the verge of tearing skin.

Not anything.

"Fuck, baby," he growled, running one of his hands down my spine. "You feel like mine."

I didn't tell him that I was his. He already knew that. He was taking me with so much intensity that he knew exactly what he had.

And then he started to move that thumb inside my ass, and I realized that that hadn't been removed either. That was explaining why I felt so full. That was also explaining why this felt so different than it usually did.

It felt right.

It felt perfect.

It felt oh, so fucking good.

Then he shocked the living shit out of me when he moved his thumb, but only long enough that he could sink two fingers inside with his cock, coating those fingers with me, and then replacing them inside my sensitive hole.

The entire thing took seconds, but it was enough to send my body to the verge of orgasm once again.

"Sweet baby Jesus," I found myself saying. "Oh, fuck."

I couldn't find the words. I didn't know what to say or think. I didn't know whether I wanted him to stop, or do more.

And lucky for me, he did know.

He knew that I didn't want him to stop.

His speed slowed, and he focused on what he was doing to my ass, letting my orgasm wane and my cognitive thinking to come back online.

"There you are," he growled, pressing against me gently.

"Did I go somewhere?" I breathed, looking at him over my shoulder. "Subspace, maybe?" I teased.

He smiled at me and then leaned forward until his mouth pressed against mine. The position was less than comfortable, but the way his lips felt on mine made me want to endure the stretch and burn in my thighs forever.

"Yeah," he growled. "I may have put you there, though."

I laughed into his mouth, and he slowly let his fingers pull from my body.

"One day, I'm going to take you there," he growled, pronouncing that with a sweep of his fingers against my anus.

I had no control of my filter, otherwise I wouldn't have said what I said right then.

"You don't have to wait until one day," I told him. "You can take me there right now."

Then I bit my lip at the way his eyes flared in appreciation.

"I do have to wait," he said, sounding somewhat forlorn. "There isn't any lube, and there's no way in hell I'll take you there the first time without it."

I pushed up, and he tightened his hold onto my hips, trying to still my movement.

"I have some."

He let me go so abruptly that I nearly impaled myself on his shaft due to the precarious balance only having one foot on the ground.

"Where?" he barked.

Then he pulled his rock-hard cock out of my pussy, and I really did feel off balance then.

"First drawer of my…" I pointed in the direction of my underwear drawer. "Underneath my thongs to the left."

He walked away, and I watched at first how his dick led the way, and then the bunch and release of the muscles of his ass as he walked.

Damn.

"Goddamn," he growled, holding up the bottle.

I didn't know why I bought it. I'd seen it one day a few months ago and had purchased it on a whim.

I'd even had to go through self-checkout with a cart full of groceries because I didn't want the male checker that was no more than nineteen to see what I'd gotten.

My cheeks heated when his lust-filled eyes met mine. "Fuckin A." He paused before he took a single step past the dresser toward where I was now standing. "You're sure?"

My entire body shivered at the way his voice sounded like he was speaking past a throat full of gravel.

"Yes," I whispered almost incoherently.

His slow grin was enough to send any sane woman running.

I wasn't sane.

I was Hannah. Thirty years old, a mom of two, and a stepmom to one. I was a nurse. A normal girl who was in love with a man that set my blood on fire, and he was asking me to do something I'd never, ever considered doing before with anyone else in my life. Not even my ex-husband.

He started coming toward me, and I moved backward.

My eyes were on the way he was moving to me, like a cat would stalk something he was about to devour. Pounce on and attack without a second's notice.

My back hit the cold wall, and I inadvertently shifted sideways, disrupting the curtains covering the window.

The curtains parted, and a shaft of light from the streetlamp outside had me turning to survey behind me.

Which was my mistake.

I wasn't prepared to find him practically on top of me when I turned back around.

I wasn't prepared for him to take my wrist into his, and then place the bottle of lube inside of my hand.

I wasn't prepared for him when he said, "Get me ready."

I didn't know what to do!

I'd never once needed lube.

Hence the reason that I squirted so fucking much out.

It wasn't a little bit. It was a lot.

Likely, I only needed the smallest of dollops.

Instead, I coated my entire palm in the stuff, pouring as much out as I would when I put lotion on my hands and forearms.

I had no clue how runny and sticky it would be, nor did I have any inkling of the mess it would make.

No, there I was, a handful of fucking lube in my palm, and I tipped it over straight onto his straining cock.

He started to laugh when it went everywhere, but he didn't correct me. Didn't stop to make a comment about how this was going to be fun to clean up. Not Travis. He just watched me, eyes full of need and lust, and allowed me to rub the clear liquid all over the length of his cock.

I was amazed with how much I had and reached my hand down to cup his balls as I continued to work his cock.

His cock felt so hard that there wasn't a single inch of softness to him. He was at least nine inches in my hand, if not more. And the thickness of that nine inches was something that I'd never forget. It filled me so amazingly. I could still practically feel him inside of me.

And that was when I started to get nervous.

If his fingers—only two—were inside of me, what would it feel like if it were his cock?

I was so lost in the way he felt in my hands that I didn't realize I was actually making him curse until he stilled both of my hands by saying, "Stop."

I stopped and looked up into his eyes and waited for his next direction.

He pulled me by the hips and settled me between his thighs. He was on the seat that took up a small alcove right in front of our window, and his back was pressed against the curtains, his thighs spread wide with his glorious balls resting between them.

His cock was jutting straight up in the air, pointing toward the ceiling, begging me to touch it.

When I went to do just that, he stilled my hand.

"Got nothing left. You touch me, I'll fucking come."

I bit my lip and dropped my hand to my side, my finger steadily tapping out a rhythm on my thigh.

"Turn around and put your knees on either side of my thighs."

I turned, and then slowly got into position, my ass hovering high over his straining erection.

My knees were digging into the outdoor swing cushion I'd gotten on sale at Lowe's last week, and from across the room, I could see myself in the mirror that hung above my dresser, the panty drawer still mostly open from where Travis had left it.

I bit my lip at the way my breasts hung, full and supple. The way my belly rose and fell with my accelerated breathing. The way I had a blush rising over my chest to my chin.

My eyes, however…those were glazed in passion.

Then I felt the tip of one finger on my anus.

I jumped.

He chuckled darkly and said, "Bend forward a little."

I did, placing both of my hands on his knees—uncaring that I was getting my lubed-up hands all over his skin.

He swirled that finger around my asshole, teasing, caressing, coaxing.

At first, I was stiff, but the longer he let his fingers move the more I relaxed, which was exactly what he wanted.

"Good," he said, then breached me.

I bit my lip and dropped my head, my blonde curls falling over my shoulder to brush against the insides of his knees.

I couldn't help myself from moving my hips, slowly at first.

God, I needed him. Needed this.

Then one finger went to two, then two to three.

He worked each inside of me slowly, getting me well acclimated before he gave me more.

And by the time I was easily taking three, my asshole stretched for his invasion, I was on the verge of another orgasm.

Travis was a good man. He never once let me come without him—but we'd only had sex a total of seven times.

Three of which had been a year ago.

The other four had been wonderful, amazing even. But they didn't feel anything like this.

Tonight, with Travis, had been a bucket list on every single woman's dream lover.

They wanted to orgasm more times than they could count. They wanted those orgasms to be immense. *Powerful.*

They wanted their man to take charge and give them exactly what they didn't know they needed.

This, well this was something I could never have dreamed up. Not in a thousand years.

And it just kept getting better and better.

"Sit back, honey."

I hesitated, but with the gentle hum of his voice, and the slight pressure of his hand on my hip—I gave him exactly what he asked for.

I lowered my ass.

He helped guide me, ensuring that I wouldn't accidentally impale myself on his length.

I didn't know much about anal sex, but I knew enough to know that it would hurt like a mother if I forced him inside of me without at least allowing myself to adjust first.

"This way you get to control everything, baby," he growled, smoothing his hand down my spine.

I finally stopped when I felt his erection prod my vagina, and he readjusted his cock, aiming it toward that forbidden hole.

The second it touched the entrance, I stilled, waiting to see what he wanted me to do next.

And he didn't disappoint.

"Your first inclination is going to be to clench," he rumbled, pressing a kiss to my spine. "I want you to push out like you are going to force it away from you."

I nodded my head, words escaping me.

We didn't speak for the next few minutes.

He may have done it out of want. I did it out of necessity since I couldn't seem to catch my breath.

"Sit down."

I did, slowly at first.

So slow, in fact, that I froze the moment that his cock head started to breach me.

"It's okay, baby."

His coaxing voice had me letting my ass fall even further, another scant half an inch.

My asshole started to burn, and I bit my lip, suddenly rethinking this whole thing.

Jesus, it hurt.

Everything inside of me screamed to sit up, to get his cock as far away from my anus as I could get it.

The other half of me, though, was so turned on it wasn't even funny.

The sharp bite of pain was intoxicating.

"Force it out of you," he murmured, letting his fingers trail around my asshole.

It felt weird. It felt, honestly, wrong.

But oh, God. Just that touch alone had my empty pussy clenching.

"Take a deep breath and let it out."

I did.

"Now push out."

I closed my eyes and did what he asked, bearing down on my lower half, pushing him out just as he asked me to.

And felt my asshole give, allowing him to sink halfway inside before I froze and locked my thighs.

"Good," he soothed, trailing his tongue along my shoulder. "Take more."

The burning wasn't so much burning anymore as it was a feeling of fullness. So full.

He pressed on my hip with the hand that wasn't rimming my asshole, and I bit my lip and gave him more.

Inch by inch he disappeared inside of me until my ass finally met his thighs, and he was all the way inside.

I was panting, pulling breaths in and out of my lungs so fast that I was on the verge of hyperventilating.

"You feel so big," I breathed through the pants. "God."

I wanted to feel him inside of me like he'd been doing, but there was so much going on in my body that I couldn't tell myself to do anything.

Luckily Travis was a little more in control of himself because he pulled my back in tight to his chest and bucked his hips up slightly.

"Feels good, though, right?"

I nodded. "Yeah."

It did. It really, really did.

Anal sex had never been on the top of my priority list, but I knew that this wouldn't be our last time. Especially with the way I was feeling.

"You ready to move?"

Oh, hell yeah, I was ready to move.

"Yesssssss," the words came out in a hiss, and I closed my eyes in complete surrender as I helped him move. My thighs screamed at the activity and the way they were being put to use.

My arms were on the tops of his knees, pushing as well. But mostly it was the way he was holding my hips and moving me up and down the length of his shaft that kept me going.

On one longer thrust, his cock slipped completely from my anus, and I moaned in dismay.

Travis didn't, though.

"Line me back up, baby."

I did, reaching backward for his cock, and lining him back up to my entrance.

"Good," he growled, then sank me back down the length of his cock.

This time, the burning stretch wasn't there, only a delicious bloom of wonder as he filled me back up.

The second that I was completely on his shaft, he spread his hand on my entire ass cheek and lifted.

How he knew that my thighs were getting more use than they'd gotten the entire day, I didn't know. But I was glad.

I vaguely wondered why he didn't keep his hands on my hips, but before the thought could fully form in my brain, he was using the other hand—the one that hadn't made an appearance in my asshole, FYI—to circle the tiny bud of my clit.

I gritted my teeth and moved, ignoring the way my thighs were crying and slammed myself back down.

That's when his fingers slipped away from my clit and filled me. Three of them, making me feel the fullest I'd ever felt.

I lost my breath in a single whoosh of exhaled air, and came, right then and there.

He cursed, not expecting it, and lost what little control he had.

His fingers inside of me, as well as the hand on my ass, helped lift me since I was rendered immobile by the orgasm that swept over me.

Then I felt Travis' cock jerking and twitching inside of my ass, and I knew subconsciously that he'd gone, too.

Yet I couldn't find it in me to care.

Not when he was making me come so hard that I wasn't sure I'd ever be the same.

My lungs screamed for air, and I gasped, my eyes snapping open, as I stared, fixated, at the now open window.

Open, as in so open that I could see out to the street, and count the number of cars that were lining it.

"Window's open," I managed to gasp.

Travis looked over my shoulder to the window that his naked back was plastered against, and grunted. "Sure the fuck is."

I rolled my eyes and leaned forward.

He went with me and let the curtains fall back into place.

"Really need to get blinds for those," he muttered. "Fucking weird shaped window with its special-order blinds."

I snickered.

Then he turned serious.

"If there is one thing you can count on in this life, it's my love for you. I may be dead and gone, but that love isn't something that will ever fade." He turned my face so that I could feel his forehead on the side of my chin. "I love you like crazy, Han. So much that I hate a man that I know is happily married. So much that when you got on his bike today, I decided that you'll never get on the back of Wolf's bike ever again. Even if he was bringing you to me."

I started to giggle as my heart filled to the brim with happiness.

"Get up, girl," he growled, depositing a kiss on my cheek before moving his hands to my hips and pushing me up.

The moment he slid from inside of me, I had a moment of panic. Things down there did not feel right, but just as quickly as I thought that the spasming of my asshole slowed, and then stopped altogether, returning to normal.

I bit my lip and turned to face him.

"Not saying that I won't do that again with you, but just sayin', it feels really weird right now."

Like very weird. The fact that his come was inside of me and couldn't escape was making for a lot of weird feelings.

"Go start the shower," he ordered. "I'm going to do a final check of the house," he said as he reached for the underwear drawer. "Then I'll join you."

And just like that he was gone, giving me what I knew was my privacy to do what I needed to do in the bathroom before he got back.

So, I did just that and didn't complain once when I saw him re-enter the bathroom and head to the shower where I was at. Nor did I complain when I saw him throw those newly-cleaned underwear on the floor in his usual pile of dirty clothes right next to the laundry hamper.

It really must be true love.

CHAPTER 24

One day I'll get my shit together. Today's not that day.
-Coffee Cup

Travis

"Hey Han, do you have any quarters?" I called. "The girls are getting Kona Icee drink slushie things today at school, and I only have six dollars. They need ten to get the color changing cup."

"In my purse!" came Hannah's yell from our bedroom where she was getting ready to go to her new job as caretaker for an elderly woman. "At the bottom under all the junk."

I scanned the kitchen counters for her purse and spotted it on top of the fridge of all places.

I walked to it and got it off, reveling in the weight of it, and opened the first compartment. Then the second. Finally, still not seeing any quarters, I spotted a somewhat hidden compartment and yanked it open.

Then I froze for all of two seconds before pulling out what I saw.

Walking with it to the bedroom, I held it up to show her.

"Since when do you carry a gun in your purse?" I asked in surprise.

Hannah looked over.

"Since I was twenty-one and could legally carry it without going to jail," she answered. "My brother made me take the concealed carry class with him when I was about three days past my twenty-first birthday."

I blinked.

Then grinned.

"That's so fuckin' hot," I told her. "Why am I just now realizing this? I've been in love with you for a year!"

She shrugged on her scrub top and sat down on the edge of the bed to put some really colorful socks that didn't match in the least on her feet.

"I think that's the point of carrying concealed, so nobody knows that you have it," she teased.

That was true.

I carried concealed, but it was kind of hard to hide something on my body when she was pressing herself against it. We'd never actually discussed my carrying—or her carrying for that matter—which was the reason I believed I didn't know that she did until now.

"Fuck me," I muttered. "I actually have a hard-on right now."

She rolled her eyes, and I winked at her before walking back to the kitchen and putting her gun back in her purse. I grinned at it wickedly before searching the other side for the loose quarters.

She had twenty-eight of them.

No joke. Twenty-eight quarters and that wasn't including the dimes, pennies, and nickels.

Once I counted out four dollars, I shoved the rest back in her purse, put it back on top of the refrigerator and split them between the two girls' bags.

"All right, girls," I told them where they were sitting on the couch. "I put your Ziploc bags on the counter with your names on them, just like you asked. I gotta go to work."

Both girls immediately jumped off the couch and ran to me.

Reggie was in a pink cotton nightgown that flowed around her ankles, while Alex was in a Star Wars flannel number that I could've sworn I'd never seen before.

They both hit me like wrecking balls and threw their arms around my waist.

My heart swelled that much further.

"Be good at school today," I told them. "You have early release, right?"

Both girls looked up at me and nodded.

God, this was what paradise felt like, wasn't it?

Dropping a kiss onto both of their foreheads, I patted them on the back and said, "Gotta go. Be good for Hannah."

Alex gave me a thumb up, and Reggie snorted. "We're always good for Mommy."

I grunted and turned to where TJ was lying in his swing.

Once I gave him a kiss, I walked back to the bedroom where I saw Hannah was now in her bathroom fixing her hair.

She had a piece of it in her hands, and she was running the straightening iron over it while looking at me in the mirror.

"You headed out?"

I nodded. "Got a pickup to do before eight. The bank said they'd give me an extra grand if I got it done today. Apparently, the guy was a dick to them when they called."

She snorted. "Nice."

I walked up to her back and tilted her head my way before laying a kiss down on the tips of her lips.

"Love you, Han."

Her eyes went soft. "I love you, too, Trav."

I left moments later but was only five minutes into my drive to work when I got the call.

"Hello?" I answered.

"Tate Casey is getting out next week."

My brows rose.

"No shit?"

"No shit," came Evander's deep reply. "Just got the call at the office. He was let out early due to good behavior. A lady friend was the one who called. She said that he'd be by sometime soon."

I found myself grinning.

"Hot damn."

Evander grunted. "Thought the same fucking thing." He paused. "You going out to the pick-up that was called in last night?"

I nodded. "Sure am. I'll be at the garage in ten. Then I'll leave straight from there. My hope is to get it knocked out before noon."

Evander grunted a reply, "See you then."

An hour later, I was standing in front of a parking garage, staring at the low clearance sign.

"Not gonna make that," I muttered to Evander.

"Nope," he agreed. "Guess we can go in there and try to pop the lock."

I shrugged.

"These newer model cars, it's possible that we won't be able to do that. But at this point, I don't think we have a choice unless we want to wait for him to leave. Which my sources say he hasn't done in a week because he thinks someone's going to 'steal his car.'"

Evander started to chuckle.

Then I started to hear sirens.

My brows furrowed as I turned to look behind me.

We were a couple blocks away from the hospital. A mile away from the interstate. But that was all in the opposite direction of where I was hearing the sirens. They were coming from the direction of the school.

"Bet that cop is sitting outside of the school again, pulling people over left and right for going a mile over the speed limit," Evander muttered.

"Old man Crew is a douche, but people should know not to speed," I pointed out, and started walking toward the building.

A feeling of unease swept over me.

I thought it had to do with the pick-up we were on. Little did I know that it had nothing to do with me, and everything to do with the girls that I loved with all my heart only a few short blocks away.

CHAPTER 25

I hope that wherever my hair ties are, that they're happy. That's all that matters.
-Hannah's secret thoughts

Hannah

I was still chuckling to myself about Travis' reaction as I dropped TJ off at daycare.

The smile was still firmly in place even when I pulled into the drop-off line at the school.

The mothers were acting extra crazy today due to it being almost the last day of school for the kids, so they were taking extra time letting their kids off, and backing the lines up almost all the way out of the school into the intersection of the highway.

I was fourteenth in line—I knew, since I'd been counting since I got into the line—and was thankful that I'd dropped TJ off first.

While I'd dropped TJ off, I'd explained that the two days following today would be his last because his grandmother was going to be watching him from now on.

When I'd texted Travis' mother for confirmation, she'd exuberantly replied with a resounding, *'Yes, absolutely, a hundred times yes!'*

Which reminded me, I had to call the bus barn and make sure that I rerouted the girls for next year, though I could probably do that with their teachers when they started school in the fall.

All of this was going through my head as I listened to the girls chatter incessantly in the back seat about what they were going to do from now on with all their free time.

Would they color in their workbooks? Would they try to figure out how to hit the ball harder next year for softball? Would their grandmother (yes, Reggie was now claiming Travis' mother as her own grandmother) take them to the city pool the first day they were off?

"Just make sure you don't wear her out too much, girls," I told them. "She also has TJ now, so it's not going to be easy for her to drop everything and do your bidding."

The girls acted like I never even spoke.

Finally, after another ten minutes in the line, we pulled up to the teachers that were helping the kids out of the cars.

The doors opened, and then both girls started to yell when they couldn't get the back hatch to open.

"Shit," I growled, grabbing my purse. "Stupid car."

The latch on the hatch was broken, and would only open if I had my keys directly next to it. I'd been needing to take it in for weeks now, but with no time to do that, and too much stress at my job and at home, I hadn't found the time.

"Sorry, sorry," I muttered to the teacher that was giving me an ugly look.

It wasn't like I was the entire reason the line was backed up. *Someone before me had to have made a mistake, too!*

Regardless, I ignored the looks and pushed the button to open the hatch.

That's when I heard the screaming.

At first, I was confused.

I was looking around at the exit of the school, wondering if a kid had tried to cross the road, and the cars hadn't stopped to let them cross. It was so bad there. Sometimes I used to drop TJ off and walk the girls across the street. When I realized that the dumbasses in our small town not only didn't follow the posted speed limit for school zones but also didn't stop to let children cross the street, I stopped walking them and started running them through the lines.

It added twenty minutes to the day, but if it were safer, then I'd do it.

But after assessing the situation, and seeing cars still pulling out, I realized that the problem wasn't down there, but up in front somewhere.

My eyes continued to move around the parking lot, looking around to see the sources of the screams.

And that was when I saw that the eyes weren't pointed somewhere else. They were pointed at me.

At me...*and my girls.*

My girls had just gotten out of the car and were standing at my side.

My eyes darted around like an addict looking for his next fix, trying to identify the danger.

My hand was already pushing on Alex's head, shoving her down hard to the ground.

Reggie, startled by this, dropped down to her knees, and I hissed at them.

I don't know what I said exactly, but they obeyed instantly.

And that's when I saw it.

Her.

Allegra.

Standing there, a gun in her hand.

I heard my brother's words in my ear.

Deep Breath. Look around. Assess the situation. Make sure the surroundings are clear. Draw. Aim. Fire. Swift. Smooth. No hesitation. Hesitation kills.

Hesitation kills.

I used to joke about that with my brother ever since he told me that phrase.

"Hesitation kills!" I used to say when he rethought turning in front of another car. "Hesitation kills!" I used to tease when he thought twice about picking up that third donut.

There was nothing funny about the situation I was facing, though.

Nothing.

The teachers that were standing on either side of my car were now hunched down by the front fender. My girls were shoved under the car—most likely by what I said.

And there Allegra stood, a shotgun pointed at me.

Just as suddenly as I identified the threat, I had a gun pointed right back at her.

My finger was already squeezing the trigger of my 9mm.

It took all of three-tenths of a second to make sure that everything was clear in front of me. There was nobody standing behind or beside her. Everyone was down and screaming.

"Put it down!"

She fired.

I pulled the trigger.

It hit her in the shoulder.

Her second shot exploded. I heard it first, then saw more than heard the glass of my windshield explode fully.

Then, almost as if she were inhuman, she started running away.

The shotgun lay on the ground where she'd once been standing.

My eyes darted around, double-checking for more threats, but there were none.

That was the day that changed my life. That was the day that I started to be proactive in protecting my children.

That was the day that would change not just my life, but many lives to come.

CHAPTER 26

I can now forget what I'm doing while I'm actually doing it.
-Text from Travis to Hannah

Travis

"Got it," Evander grunted, attaching the last chain. "You want me to go ahead and deliver it straight to the bank?"

I nodded my head. "Yea. It's getting on up there in time…"

My phone rang, and I winced when I saw the screen.

I held up my hand at Evander. "Go, I gotta take this."

I didn't want to take this, but I had to.

Evander gave me a lazy wave and then got into the truck and drove off all before I could say another word.

Wiping the sweat off my forehead—we pushed the fucking car all the way out of the garage from the top floor—I answered it with a terse, "Hello?"

"Travis?"

I'd heard Allegra crying all of four times in my life, so to hear her actively bawling, and sounding like she was in pain, it made me stop for a few moments.

"Yeah?" I asked warily.

"Something bad happened to me," she sniffled. "And I need to tell you something."

Need to tell me something?

“What?” I asked, wondering if what she had to tell me was related to how fucked up and stupid she was for having driven my child in a car with her while she was drunk off her ass.

“I’m sick,” she coughed. “And I want to give you some papers.”

“What kind of papers?”

I heard her moan.

“Papers that give up my rights as a parent,” she hesitated. “I know that what I did was wrong. I shouldn’t have pursued custody in court, and I think it’s time that I leave. Leave this town, and never come back.”

That made me angry.

“And what about Alex?” I growled.

“Alex is safer without me around. I’m not in a good place. I’ve done some…things,” she hedged.

Some things.

I didn’t want to know what ‘things’ she’d done.

Not at all.

But I sensed that if she didn’t meet with me, she’d be gone for good, and I would forever be waiting for the other shoe to drop when it came to her.

So, I agreed to meet.

“Fine,” I said. “Where do you want to meet?”

“Your house?”

I snorted. “Definitely not.”

She made a frustrated noise. “How about mine?”

That wouldn’t be happening either.

"I'll be at the office in ten. We can meet in the parking lot there."

It was only a few blocks away, and it was as neutral as it could get in a town this small with people that made it a living to butt into everyone else's business.

"Okay," she said. "I'll be there in about a minute and a half."

I rolled my eyes. "I'll get there when I get there."

She said something else, but I'd already hit the 'END' call button and shoved it into my pocket.

Then I thought better of it, remembering my fight with Hannah last night, and pulled it back out to call her.

She didn't answer, though.

So I left a voicemail and got into my truck.

It took me eight to get back to the shop, but only because it seemed like every single officer in the county was now on their way to a scene.

Making a mental note to turn my radio onto scan once Allegra was through with whatever bullshit she had to give me so I could figure out what in the hell was going on, I pulled into the parking lot of my business and parked in one of the bays.

Once I had it where I wanted it, I shut the truck off and got out, looking around at all the trucks that were supposed to be there today that weren't.

There was only one tow truck in the bay today, and that was one that was meant to be serviced.

Hell, even the service guys weren't around.

Where the hell was everyone at?

"There you are," I heard Allegra's voice come from behind the truck.

I turned, took one step, and felt the most searing pain I'd ever felt hit my chest.

I heard the roar of the shotgun just as my head hit the concrete.

I'd fallen.

I'd hit the ground so hard that I was having trouble breathing.

Or was it because I'd been hit in the chest by something?

My brain was fuzzy, and I couldn't make sense of things.

Allegra? Had Allegra hit me with something?

***

Baylor

I grunted as I pulled the last of the chains off the truck.

Today was normally the day that I'd be off, but since we were short staffed, I'd come in anyway.

Now I was having to deal with this bullshit.

"Listen," the woman whose car I was repossessing pleaded, "if you take the car, I have no way to get to work.

I looked over at her, then dropped down to my knees and started to crawl under the car to attach the chains.

They weren't needed, not with today's technology and advances when it came to towing, but I was old school. I liked them on there because it made me feel better, so sue me.

That's when I felt something on my foot.

I looked down at the woman—girl really. What was she, all of twenty-one?

"Don't touch me," I ordered.

I hated being touched. Fuck, that was why I hadn't had sex in over eight years.

I was seriously on the verge of kicking out with my foot when she let go, then fell to her ass in defeat.

"Perfect," she whispered.

That's when the tears started to drip out of her eyes.

Fuck!

I hated when women cried. Especially pretty ones.

Shit, fuck, damn.

I attached the chain and scooted out from under the car, not bothering to dust the dirt and grass off my back. This wasn't the first time today I got on the ground, and wouldn't be the last. That I knew for sure.

If I wasn't repossessing a car, I'd be towing a truck to either A, the impound yard. B, an auto mechanic, or C, a body specialist to get repair work done due to a wreck.

Not all of my pick-ups were repossessions.

And most of them didn't come with crying women. The majority of them came with little to no trouble at all, but if there was trouble, I preferred it in the form of a man swinging his fist at my face instead of tears.

But that's just me.

I lived for the adrenaline spikes that this job offered me.

"Come on, darlin'." I held out my hand. "I'll take you where you need to go."

She looked around the parking lot—the mall parking lot—and swallowed.

She didn't take my hand.

"That's okay," she whispered. "I'll walk. I've done it before, and I'll do it again."

I didn't get a chance to say anything before my phone rang.

When I pulled it out of my pocket and placed it to my ear, the woman was already slinking away, her head hung.

I resisted the urge to wrap my arms around her shoulder—because goddamn I did not need another crying woman on my hands—and answered the phone.

"Yo."

"Get down here now."

"Tate?" I asked.

Before I could reply, he said, "Shop." And then hung up.

I didn't even look back at the woman as I dove for the open door of my truck.

If Tate was out, and he said to get to the shop now, then something was seriously wrong.

Five minutes of bat-shit-out-of-hell driving later, I arrived at the shop and pulled into the parking lot just in time to see Tate Casey, my best friend, and the man that'd been in jail for what felt like forever, aim a gun at the back of Allegra's body, and pull the trigger.

She fell like a rock, clutching her arm.

When she scooted around and went to turn to see what had hit her, Tate stepped behind the rack of tires, and I bailed out of my truck.

I took the gun from my friend, the one that normally hung in Travis' office, and looked at him with confusion clouding my eyes.

That was until I saw my brother on the floor, blood pooling around him on the dirty bay floor, with a hole in his chest. Well, a lot of them.

That was likely due to the shotgun discarded haphazardly at Allegra's feet.

"Fuck, man," I groaned. "Get the fuck out of here. Don't come back for a few days."

When I turned to make sure Tate complied, he was already gone.

CHAPTER 27

Nutritional Labels should also include a 'what if I ate the whole fucking box' section.
-Hannah's secret thoughts

Hannah

I'd forgotten.

I'd been very careful not to drive onto school property with my gun in my car.

I'd park at the daycare and walk the kids over while leaving it in the car—but then I'd witnessed a driver nearly plow into me and the girls, and I'd stopped walking them over.

Today? *It was raining.* Today? *I'd dropped them off directly in front of the school.*

I'd never once intended to get out of the car, but my back hatch wouldn't open. I had to get out, and I had to have my keys. I thought it'd be easier to get the purse and just use the key fob's closeness to the tailgate to open it, rather than pulling the keys out.

It wasn't intentional to have my gun out of my car at all.

A gunman walked onto school property and immediately started opening fire on me…on my girls.

At first, I wasn't sure what the hell was going on.

The screams.

I didn't think. I just reacted.

I pulled my gun out of my purse, aimed, and fired.

"You didn't think to look around to make sure that nobody else was in the line of fire?"

My eyes flicked up to the man questioning me.

I nodded my head. "I did. I gauged that no one else was around…I opened fire on her."

I was explaining my reasoning for having a gun on school property, and it wasn't going so well.

I'd been questioned for going on two hours now, and the angry-eyed officer—FBI agent—was staring at me like I was already tried and convicted in his book.

"You gauged that no one else was around," he drawled like he didn't believe me.

I nodded.

"Yes," I agreed almost immediately. "I looked, saw that there was nobody behind her but a brick building that I knew that my bullets wouldn't penetrate, and fired."

"How did you know that the bullets wouldn't penetrate?" he pushed, clearly not believing that I knew what I was talking about.

"I've already told you that my brother is a police officer. He's on the SWAT team. When I spoke with him about what bullets to put in the gun, he instructed me to buy hollow point bullets."

"Hollow points aren't guaranteed not to penetrate a wall," he chided as if he were instructing a small child.

I was getting upset at this point.

"No, you're exactly right," I agreed. "However, if you hit what you're aiming at, it shouldn't be a problem."

I'd surprised him, that I could tell.

"Well, Ms…"

Some sort of commotion at the door had us both looking up, and a furious Baylor was standing there.

"Get up, you're going with me." He pointed directly at my chest.

"I'm sorry, Sir." The agent stood up. "But we're not finished here."

Baylor looked at the man like he was a speck of dirt on a white shirt. As if it didn't belong anywhere near his vicinity.

"I'm sorry, Sir," Baylor said back, just as controlled. "But you've had her in here for over two hours. You haven't given her a phone call. You haven't arrested her. You haven't given her access to a lawyer. And again, you haven't arrested her, so as far as I'm concerned, she's free to go."

"Then I'll arrest her," the agent stated, sounding full of authority.

My belly dropped.

"You have no reason to arrest her," Baylor snapped. "She was defending her child. You can charge her with a crime, yes, but then you'll have every single senator and Republican, as well as parent in this county, upset that you did because she was protecting *children*."

The agent's lips thinned.

"Her husband-to-be has been shot," Baylor hissed. "He's in surgery, and she needs to be there, and not here."

"How was he shot?" the agent asked at the same time that I shrieked, "What?"

It was high-pitched, hysterical, and from the very bottom of my heart as I let those words take root.

Her husband-to-be has been shot.

What. The. Fuck.

I got up and started toward the door.

“I’ll be there to arrest her in two hours,” the agent instructed Baylor.

I didn’t say another word as I ran out of the room and straight out of the police station.

I didn’t look at the men and women that were there, filing their own statements.

I ran and didn’t stop until I reached the tow truck that Baylor usually drove around.

It had the number ‘9’ on it and had fuzzy dice hanging from the rearview mirror.

“What happened?” I gasped, looking at Baylor.

“Buckle up,” he ordered.

I could tell he wouldn’t leave the parking lot until I did, so I reached behind my shoulder blindly, latched onto the belt, and roughly yanked it over my body.

***

I stood over Travis’ bed and stared down at his chest.

It was covered with fifteen pieces of gauze, all dotting from his clavicle to his belly button, and everywhere in between.

“Shot him from pretty far away,” the doctor said. “Could’ve been a lot worse. As it is, the pellets only penetrated about an inch into his skin, all the way around. As long as he gives it a few weeks, he’ll recover just fine. But that means zero movement. I don’t want him doing anything but getting up to go to the bathroom. Showers are out until the wounds heal for a few days. Possibly a week. He can take a bath with the tub filled about half full. No submerging anything until then."

I listened to the doctor explain what had happened and how the next few weeks would be for Travis, who was still heavily sedated.

I stared at the pieces of gauze. Fifteen. Fifteen places that a pellet had penetrated his beautiful chest. A beautiful chest that would forever be marred.

"What happened to Allegra?" I whispered.

"Shot in both shoulders, believe it or not. Not dead."

I looked over to find Baylor standing there, his arms crossed over his chest, muscles bulging as he tried to hold in the urge to do something. *Punch someone.*

"Which room?"

"Don't."

I looked over to find Travis' eyes open and staring at me with a glaze to them.

"Trav," I whispered, taking a few quick steps forward.

Before I could touch him, however, there was a commotion at the door.

"Hannah Morton?"

I gritted my teeth.

I hated that I still had Joshua's last name. I'd taken the step to change my name back to my maiden name, but then I'd met Travis. My hopes had heightened, and I thought it would be odd to change my name in case something more came of us.

So I'd left it alone.

Now I wished I'd changed it.

"Yeah?"

That's when I saw the agent, as well as two uniformed officers, standing at the door.

One of them had cuffs in his hand.

"You're under arrest for…"

There was a roaring in my ears, and I closed my eyes in defeat.

Rough hands went around my wrists, and I was turned to face the bed where Travis was looking at me with horror in his eyes.

He started to get up, putting his hands on the bed where the white handles were, and I shook my head at him frantically.

"Don't move!" I ordered. He stopped at my forceful tone. "Don't do it. Don't move. Be good."

Travis opened his mouth, but before he could say another word, I was taken away.

Arrested.

Son. Of. A. Bitch.

I'd lose my nursing license.

I'd lose my concealed carry.

Fuck, fuck, fuck.

My girls, however, were alive. Was I really losing here?

CHAPTER 28

Shhh, my coffee cup and I are having a moment. Come back later.
-Coffee Cup

Michael

I stomped up the steps of the police station—a sorry excuse for one, if my opinion was asked.

It wasn't, but still.

"Where is Hannah Morton?"

That was asked to the first officer I found, which happened to be a woman who looked like she was afraid of just about anything—loud sounds, small dogs, rabbits. Possibly gerbils.

"Ummm," she hesitated. "She's in the cell in back."

I passed her.

"Sir, you can't go back there."

I ignored her.

I had to make sure that she was okay before I found whatever motherfucker that'd arrested her, and gave him a piece of my mind.

It didn't take me long to find her.

Hostel, Texas wasn't a very big place, so it was no surprise that there were only two cells in the entire place.

At least they put my sister in a cell all by herself. If they'd put her in there with that drunk motherfucker that I could smell from the goddamn doorway, I'd have been pissed.

"Hannah Banana?"

Hannah was leaning forward, her hands on her knees, her feet planted on the floor. Her head was hung, and I could tell without actually seeing or hearing the words leaving her lips that she was saying something over and over in her head.

Her head snapped up, and she was on her feet in an instant.

"Is Travis okay?"

I nodded. "Yeah, from what I hear."

Her eyes closed, and tears started to slip down her cheeks.

"Han."

She opened her eyes, and they were swimming with tears.

"Thank God," she said. "Did you go check on the girls?"

I nodded. "That I did. Travis' mother has them. As well as TJ."

She looked away, and I saw her throat work as she swallowed.

"You did good."

Her eyes came back to mine.

"I did?"

I nodded. "You sure the fuck did."

She looked startled at the vehemence in my voice.

"You did what you were supposed to do. You did what the Second Amendment was designed for. You protected yourself and your girls. I don't care if you broke the law doing it. I don't care if you did it on purpose. I only care that, at the end of the day, you're all right. Those girls are all right, and that you're going to see tomorrow breathing."

She blew out a breath.

"I got an update on Travis about twenty minutes ago," Hannah informed me. "They told me that Allegra shot him in the chest in the middle of the truck bay at work. When I left him at the hospital, he was so out of it, but he tried to follow me."

I nodded. "They did. When I got the call, they gave me the same info."

Her brows rose.

"Who called you?"

My lip twitched. "Travis' brother." I paused. "And then Wolf."

Hannah's brows rose.

"Really?"

I nodded. "Really."

She whistled. "Wolf heard how?"

I shrugged. "Don't know. The law enforcement community is tight-knit. Whatever happened, it was inevitable that I'd hear about it since you're my sister. Wolf probably has a few of his buddies watching out for you as well."

Her smile was small, but there.

"Will you go check on him for me?" she pleaded.

I touched her cheek through the bars. “You bet.”

Her shoulders slumped. “Thank you, Mikey Mike.”

“Be good.” I winked at her and left, not stopping until I found the piece of shit that’d arrested her.

The FBI agent that was staring at me knowingly. As if he’d assumed that I’d be looking for him.

“That was a courtesy that won’t be offered again,” the man said.

I smiled. “Is it now?”

His eye twitched.

“Let me tell you something, Agent Arrogant.”

The agent’s eyes widened. “I know a lot of people. Good and bad. Hannah? She’s not a bad person.” He opened his mouth to say something, but I interrupted. “I know that you’re a good agent. I also know that you have the authority to charge her, which you won’t be doing.”

His mouth twitched in an almost smile. “I won’t?”

I shook my head. “No, you won’t. But you gotta make it look good, I understand.”

The agent’s eyebrows rose. “You do that. Keep her for a little while, make everyone think that she’s in a lot of trouble, but I also want you to be careful here. Your story’s known.”

The man’s eyes changed, but the rest of him didn’t.

“I know about the little girl you lost. In Sandy Hook. I know, and I won’t say anything.”

Wolf had called me the minute that he’d heard that this particular agent was here. He’d then given me all the details on him and then gave his two cents on the matter.

The agent swallowed, showing emotion now.

"And if I were you, I'd be really careful about what you do."

We both knew what I meant.

School shooters that had the unfortunate luck to run into this agent normally had some bad stuff happen to them.

Bad stuff that left them little more than a shell.

As much as I was all right with this bitch who'd shot at my sister being a 'shell,' I was not okay with my sister going down because he'd fucked up and gotten a little too creative. Hannah wasn't going down because this guy was on a revenge mission for every single school shooter that ever lived.

But I knew in the next instant that there wouldn't be any misunderstandings between us because this agent had his shit together.

"I'll be back to get her in a few hours. Try to make it before dinner so they don't have to eat without her."

The man nodded once. "Be back around four."

And I left and didn't look back.

***

Travis looked like shit.

He had bruising all over his chest, and it went all the way up to his neck and disappeared into his beard.

"You look like shit."

Travis grunted, not opening his eyes as he did.

"She okay?" he rasped.

I stared at him and waited for him to look at me before I replied.

"For some unknown reason, she's worried as hell about you."

He made a sound under his breath. "Imagine that."

I rolled my eyes. "So I hear that your ex-wife is in the room next door."

That got his attention.

His eyes narrowed, and I swear, had the side rails been up on his bed—why they weren't I quickly realized was because he'd have used them—then he'd have been up and out of that bed.

"Thanks a lot."

I turned to find another of his brothers, Baylor, standing there.

"What?" I asked.

"Been keeping that secret for the last four hours. He's hell on wheels wanting to get to Hannah, and then you have to go and mention that," Baylor grunted.

I shrugged. "If it makes you feel better," I returned my eyes to Travis, who was staring at me with an angry intensity I'd never seen in him before. "She has three armed guards, and your brother standing outside her room making sure she's not going anywhere."

Travis shook his head. "Not really."

My lips quirked. "Hmm."

He flipped me off. "Go get my girl. Then go take care of the girls."

"Done and done," I said. "Your mom has the girls, and Hannah's getting out by four."

"How do you know that?" Baylor asked before Travis could.

"I stopped by on the way here. Seems like you have a friend…one that is pretty good to have on your side if you ask me."

Baylor looked at me with eyebrows raised.

"Wolf called," I started, causing both Baylor and Travis to groan. "Said that this agent had a kid. Five and a little bit. Was lost in that school shooting a few years ago right before Christmas…remember?"

Baylor lost his scowl, and now he just looked sad.

"Could've been my girls."

I looked over to where Travis, face white as the sheet he was lying on, was watching me intently.

I nodded. "But it wasn't."

He closed his eyes. "Thanks to Hannah."

"Yeah," I agreed. "Thanks to Hannah."

Travis held out his hand. "Got a lot of things to thank you for."

I took that hand being careful not to pull the IV that was sticking out of it and shook it.

"You do," I agreed. "And as long as you take care of her, you'll repay it."

That's when his hand went limp.

I looked over to see Baylor standing next to Travis' morphine pump.

"Stubborn fucker won't do it himself."

I grinned.

"Why does that not surprise me?"

CHAPTER 29

Autocorrect makes me say things Nintendo.
-Text from Travis to Hannah

Travis

"Do you have any threes?"

My eyes peeled open, and the first thing I noticed was that I hurt.

Oh, God did I hurt.

I licked my dry, cracked lips and turned my head, a wave of nausea rising in my gut because of the pain.

"Go Fish," Hannah giggled, smiling brightly. "Alex, do you have any fours?"

"Ummmm," Alex hedged.

I started to laugh and immediately regretted it.

"Daddy!"

"Travis!"

"Travis!"

Then suddenly I had three gorgeous women surrounding me.

"Hey," I croaked.

My eyes went from Reggie's, to Alex's, and finally to Hannah's.

"Everything okay?"

All three of them nodded.

"Mommy said that you were hurt." Reggie leaned forward until her face was less than an inch from mine. "You don't look hurt."

I grinned and lifted my hand to curl around her neck, then pulled her the rest of the way down so I could place a kiss on her forehead.

"Good," I grunted. "I'm okay."

Hannah snorted, and I let Reggie go.

Alex then threw her arms around my neck and buried her face in my chest.

I saw stars.

However, I didn't pull away, and Hannah didn't stop Alex, even though Hannah could tell that she'd hurt me.

"I'm okay, baby."

Alex brought her head up.

"I'm sorry for all the mean things I said to you, Daddy. I didn't mean them."

I watched as her face crumpled, and it was all I could do not to wrap my arms around her and hold her to me.

The only thing that stopped me from doing it was something on my right side holding my arm in place.

I tried to move it, and an annoyed grunt followed.

"Oh, sorry," Hannah said, walking around the bed.

"No, don't," I told her. "Leave him there."

My eyes traveled down to my leg where TJ was sleeping between a pillow stuffed next to the rails, and my thigh.

His reassuring heat had me breathing a sigh of contentment despite the pain in my chest from where I could feel Alex's weight touching.

"Alex, did you want to show your daddy your report card?"

My stomach tensed, this time for different reasons.

Alex had been on the verge of failing school for most of the year. I wasn't sure that I *wanted* to see her grades.

But the way Alex pushed off of me with an excited cry and then ran to the corner of the room where her backpack was, had me thinking it was good news—otherwise she wouldn't be so excited.

And then when she shoved the blue paper into my face, so close to my nose that I could see nothing but blurred dots, let me know that in all likelihood, she'd passed.

Alex never wanted to show me her report card.

Never.

"You pass, baby?" I questioned.

Hannah started to laugh and pulled the paper back, allowing my eyes to focus.

My eyes went through the seventies, one sixty, and a fifty, all the way to the end, and what I saw was surprising.

"You made a hundred in all your classes this six weeks?"

"She even beat me," Reggie said, sounding proud of that fact.

I grinned and brought my hand up to Alex's face. "Good job, honey."

Alex looked so proud. "Next year, I'm going to make all A's."

I ran my thumb over her cheek, happy to see that not a single scratch or hair was misplaced on her head, and I owed that all to one woman.

"Y'all think you can go find Uncle Baylor and ask him to take you down to the cafeteria for a while?" I asked.

Now that the pain meds that my brothers had been slipping me throughout the day had cleared, my brain was back online.

Reggie started to clap.

"They have really good cinnamon rolls here!" she declared.

How she knew that, I didn't know, but I was going to ask to try one tomorrow morning.

For now, I really needed to speak to her mother.

"Aces!" Alex cried, then both children were out the door.

I could hear my brother's voice, so I wasn't worried that he'd let them go by themselves, but Hannah left anyway just to check.

I chose that moment to place my hand on my chest and look down at my sleeping son.

A sleeping son who was asleep instead of screaming at, I looked up at the clock, seven o'clock in the evening.

"He's not crying."

Hannah grinned. "No, he sure isn't."

I grinned and held out my hand.

"Wonder why?"

She took my hand and brought it up to her face. "Don't know." She paused. "And honestly, I hope that it's going to be recurring."

I agreed.

"Han?"

I swept my thumb over her chin.

"Yeah?"

"Come here."

Hannah's face broke out into a smile. Then she leaned forward and placed her mouth gently onto mine.

I kissed her, and then pressed my forehead to hers.

"Thank you."

Her eyes opened, and she pulled back slightly. "For what?"

My mouth tipped up into a smile.

"For saving my life."

She opened her mouth to disagree, and I stopped her.

"You may not think so, but you did," I interrupted her. "You saved Alex. You saved Reggie. You saved you."

Her mouth closed with an audible snap.

"That woman next door…"

Her brows furrowed in confusion.

"Allegra. She's in the room next door."

Hannah's eyes narrowed, and I kind of loved the way she got all protective.

"Don't."

Hannah's eyes lit. "You can't…"

"I know I can't," I agreed. "But for now, just stay with me."

She sighed and planted her butt on the bed next to my calf. I kept hold of her hand, though.

"She could've taken a lot of stuff away from me today," I said. "Then I'd be an empty hull like Dante."

She looked away. "I know how he feels now. Just thinking about how close I came…it's a scary fucking experience."

And it was.

I'd had plenty of time to think about what I'd heard Hannah had done, and each and every time I did, it was enough to send my heart into overdrive.

Just the thought of losing them was enough to send bile rushing up my throat.

And speaking of the devil.

I looked up to find Dante standing there, his eyes on me.

"You okay?"

I swallowed and nodded.

"Good."

Then he was gone.

CHAPTER 30

And then Satan said, 'Put the alphabet in math...'
-Coffee Cup

Dante

The moment that I made sure Travis was okay, I walked next door.

There were no guards there any longer, and with Baylor otherwise occupied with the girls, it left me with plenty of time to do what needed to be done.

I pushed through the closed door and gritted my teeth when Allegra's exhausted face turned to me.

She had two arms in casts, and her face was haggard.

"What are you…"

I held my hand up and walked further inside.

"You fucked up," I said, walking closer.

Her mouth pinched.

"What are you even doing here?" she snarled. "I thought you were out, mourning your kids."

A year ago, when it had all happened, that would've gutted me—being reminded of them.

Now I was empty, though. Nothing left inside but an empty husk of my former self.

Nothing inside of me was there any longer to get hurt.

"I'm here because you thought it'd be okay to shoot at my brother, my almost sister-in-law, and my nieces."

She scoffed.

"I didn't kill them."

My mouth fell open.

"You didn't kill them?"

I turned to find Hannah standing at the door, her eyes angry.

"Exactly." Allegra turned and sneered, pointing her anger at the newcomer. "I didn't kill them."

Before Hannah could reply, I held my hand up and silenced her.

"Wasn't really wanting witnesses for this," I said as I walked toward the bed.

That was when Allegra started to look nervous.

She scooted back in the bed as far she could go, but it wasn't far enough.

My hand closed around Allegra's throat.

"There's a payment needed here," I said very quietly. "You need to either go down for your sins or I'll take you down my own way. Which way is it going to be?"

Allegra's eyes were freaked, and I could tell that she didn't want to answer me.

She did, though.

"I'll admit to everything," she said. "I'm sor-sorry."

I laughed in her face and let her go. "Sorry isn't good enough."

I could still feel her throat in my hand.

It was intoxicating, not giving a fuck.

I no longer had a conscience.

I could literally do anything, and not feel one single regret.

"Make sure you do. Or I'll be back."

Then I left, walking around a surprised Hannah, and left not just the room, but the hospital and Hostel altogether.

***

Hannah

I watched him leave with surprise.

I'd come over here with the intentions of doing something very similar. However, Dante had gotten things across loud and clear.

Shooting Allegra a smug look, I walked away knowing that Allegra would do the only thing she could.

Admit to her sins.

CHAPTER 31

Some days the supply of available curse words is insufficient.
-Hannah's secret thoughts

Hannah

"She's working out?" I asked.

"Yes, she's doing so great," Carol Marks said. "Thank you so much for recommending her. I can feel my strength returning already."

I smiled into the phone, but only halfway.

My heart was still hurting, and Travis was still in the hospital.

I was worked to the bone.

The day that I'd been freed from jail, I'd gone to see Travis.

Once I'd ascertained that Travis would be okay, I'd then gone to work helping Baylor keep Hail Auto Recovery afloat.

Apparently, without Travis, things went downhill fast.

He was the one with the passwords. The contacts. The person that answered all emails, as well as made sure that the lights stayed on by paying bills.

Travis helped, working as much as he could from the hospital bed, but there wasn't much he could do without the essentials, like a computer and a phone that were connected to his business.

"Anyway, I just wanted to call and let you know how miraculous this has been. Thank you again."

"All right, have a good day. See you soon!"

Just when I hung up there was a knock at the door.

I looked up, and spied the man through the glass door.

Getting up, I walked to it warily and opened it.

"Can I help you?" I asked.

It was Sunday, and the office was usually closed. There'd been so much to do, however, that I'd had to come in and pay a few bills, as well as return a few phone calls.

I'd never known how much pressure Travis had been under until I'd tried to fill his shoes.

Boy, did I have some groveling to do.

"Yeah," the man looked around. "Travis in?"

I shook my head.

"Dante?"

I grimaced. "No."

He frowned.

"I'm Travis' fiancée, and I'm helping him out for a few weeks. Is there anything I can help you with?"

His eyes took me in, roaming over me from the top of my head to the tips of my toes.

"I'm Tate Casey."

EPILOGUE

I know I'm a handful, but that's why you have two hands.
-Hannah to Travis

Hannah

Thump thump.

I waited, very still, as I strained my ears.

"Where is he?"

That whispered reply came from the man at my side.

I turned over and looked at my husband, who still had his eyes closed.

As if he were going to go back to sleep.

I nearly laughed.

"My guess?" I asked, snuggling closer to him. "He's either walking into the room with Alex or Reggie."

"Let's hope."

Let's hope was right. The last time we'd thought he'd gone into the room with the girls, he'd actually been outside playing with the dog. In the mud.

I snorted and rolled over, making my way to stand.

I didn't get but half an inch in the upright position before a solid arm locked around my waist and hauled me back.

He maneuvered me into the bed, pressing his hips up against mine.

That's when I felt the nudge of his cock.

"Travis," I whispered.

Before I could say a word, he was pushing my panties down around my ankles, and rolling me over to my belly.

In the next ten seconds, I felt him part both of my knees with his, spreading me open wide for his body to wiggle in between.

Before I could say anything else, he had me up on my knees, and he was fitting his cock to my entrance.

I was ready for him, just like I always was.

We did this a lot, this quick roll in the sheets before all three kids would be up, and our chance would be gone until they were securely in bed twelve hours later.

We had to be spontaneous since we now had three very active children who felt it was their God-given right to walk in on us whenever they felt like it.

That'd been when we'd started to lock our door.

We loved our children. We loved them more than anything, but in the last eighteen months, we'd realized rather quickly that sometimes mommies and daddies needed to feel a connection that had nothing to do with their kids.

The moment that TJ had started to sleep through the night, we'd closed and locked our door for the first time.

I smiled as the memory took hold.

***

8 months ago

"You sure that it'll be okay to lock the door?" I asked nervously.

Travis ran his hand down my naked backside.

"Would you sleep naked if it were unlocked?"

I didn't even need a half a second to answer him.

"No," I said.

He snorted.

"We have an alarm. They won't get outside, and nothing can come in without us knowing. We have a baby monitor that covers all three kids' rooms. And let's not forget to mention your super human hearing."

I snorted.

I did have that.

I always knew when TJ was up since he'd been born, and now my paranoia had me listening and waking up for almost anything.

Though, Travis had that, too.

Since he'd been taken by surprise by Allegra, he'd changed.

He'd become a lot more cautious with almost everything.

Doors were always locked if we were inside. Cameras were set up in the shop. Kids taught to be aware of their surroundings.

"Where are you?"

I turned and buried my face into Travis' chest, feeling the raised scar from where one of the pellets had entered his chest.

If he'd been standing closer…if Allegra had been closer…if…

"You're lost again, baby," Travis murmured.

I felt his chest vibrate against my face, and I turned to place my lips on the scar.

"Just thinkin'," I told him. "I don't like it."

He chuckled.

"I know you don't, baby," he said. "But they're not bad."

I'd asked him to get the scars removed, but he wore them like a badge of honor.

And also as a reminder. Of not just how close he'd come to losing his life, but also how close we'd come to losing him.

"They're terrible," I countered. "But they're also you. I love every part of you."

He rolled until I was underneath him, and then pulled me until my ass was up in the air.

He smoothed his hand down my backside, dragging his nails along the smooth skin and leaving what I knew were marks.

With the lights off, however, I wouldn't be able to see them, and neither would he.

But we could feel.

I could imagine what they looked like, and the image turned me on beyond belief.

"You gonna let it go?" he asked, rubbing lightly on one cheek, and then moving to the other.

I snorted. "Never."

He smacked my ass, just this side of almost too much, and made my breath catch in my throat.

"Travis!" I gasped.

His darkly erotic chuckle filled the air.

"You know how two days ago when we were watching that porn..."

"It wasn't a porn!" I said. "It was a really popular movie."

"We were watching that porno, and I asked if you'd ever wanted to be spanked?" he continued as if I'd never contradicted him.

I snorted. "Yeah."

"I've been curious," he said, running just the top of one single finger over where he'd just smacked me a good one. "What else turns you on?"

I didn't hesitate. Didn't stop to think. Just said what I said, and knew it to be the entire, one hundred percent, God's honest truth.

"You," I said. "You could decide that you wanted to fuck me on a table full of pizza, with cheese and marinara running down my ass crack, and I'd think it was fuckin' sexy."

He started to laugh and then dropped a kiss on my back, right above the top of my ass.

"Good to know if I ever get a pizza fetish, that you're in," he teased.

Then our words were lost as he started to run his fingers down the length of my exposed sex.

This going to bed with no underwear on likely would have its benefits.

***

I moaned into my pillow when he squeezed my ass.

There would be no spanking today because spanking equaled out of control Hannah, and I didn't want to be making any noise. Because noise then equaled kids that thought we were awake.

No, today was all about that quick release, and the way Travis started taking me, hard and deep, let me know that immediately.

"Jesus, you feel so good."

I bit my lip and closed my eyes, letting the pound of his hips take me away, lull me into that space that put me well on the way to orgasm.

"So sweet," he whispered, running his thumb down the swell of my ass to come into contact with the side of my entrance.

He swept some of our combined wetness up, and then I felt him move.

The next second, I heard him lick his fingers, releasing them with a soft pop.

"So, fucking, sweet." He pronounced each word with a thrust and grind of his hips.

I found myself smiling into my pillow, teeth gritting slightly when I felt the roll of my orgasm start to sweep through me.

And then it was there, all without Travis touching me at all.

Him and his magic cock.

It was always like that with us, explosive and fast.

The only time it lasted more than twenty minutes—or even ten—was when we'd both just come, and were going at it for a second time.

I fucking loved it.

I loved it even more when I felt him stiffen behind me, and then buck his hips hard, releasing into my warm depths.

Hot splashes of come filled me as my pussy convulsed around him.

I reached between my legs and cupped his balls, my fingers skimming over the tiny scar that was the aftermath of his vasectomy from a month ago.

No, there would be no more little Hannah and Travis babies running around, and that was okay with us.

We loved our children, and although more would've been great, we felt that our family was perfect at three.

So he'd gone and fixed himself so I didn't have to, and we'd enjoyed the hell out of it since.

When the last jerks of his cock subsided, he squeezed both of my hips tightly once, and then leaned over to the side of the bed where we now kept our towels for this exact reason.

After offering me the towel, I cupped it between my legs and sighed when he pulled himself free.

That's the second that I heard the doorknob rattle with an impatient twenty-month-old's annoyed cry following shortly after.

"Dwink!"

I started to laugh and climbed to my feet beside the bed, then hurried into the bathroom and shut the door.

As I took care of my own needs, I listened to Travis dress, and then open the door for his son.

After saying a few low words to him that I couldn't hear, he'd disappeared down the hallway, leaving me to get dressed from there.

By the time I arrived in the living room, not only our kids and Travis were there, but so were his parents, two of his brothers, and Evander.

I rolled with it but stopped next to Travis with a raised brow.

He chuckled and pulled me against his bare chest.

He was dressed in jeans only. Ones that rode low on his hips, and sagged, allowing me to see every single dip, arch, and valley of his tight belly.

Oh, and let's not forget feel it.

"Seriously, would it kill y'all to stop touching each other?"

I looked over to where Baylor stood, watching us with annoyance.

"Sure, Baylor," I teased. "It might very well."

He rolled his eyes skyward.

"Did Travis tell you why we were here?"

I shook my head, and was about to reply with a 'no,' but was interrupted by a tiny force hitting my legs.

I looked down at my son and grinned before letting go of Travis to reach for him.

TJ had other things on his mind, and those involved his daddy and the cup he was holding.

"Mine!"

TJ jumped, making it about an inch off the ground.

Travis raised his brows at our little man and growled.

"Use your manners."

TJ scowled at him.

"Oh, come on, Dad."

Michael came into my kitchen moments later, his wife and children trailing in behind him.

I grinned and threw my arms around my brother, squeezing his neck as tight as I could causing him to make a choking sound.

"Jesus, Han."

Nikki laughed and slapped her hand against my brother's back.

"You remember when you said your sister was nice to Nico just a few days ago?"

I started to giggle.

Nico was Nikki's brother, and apparently, they'd been arguing about Nikki and I again.

"I take it back," Michael teased.

I rolled my eyes.

"What is everyone doing here?" I asked.

Not that I cared that they were all here, but it was seven-thirty in the morning on a Saturday.

"We're going to the lake," my brother said, brandishing a box of donuts from behind his back.

How the hell had he kept those hidden?

Nikki produced another two boxes and a bag of what looked like ten dozen donut holes.

"Ohhh," Alex cried, picking up a bag that Nikki had handed her. "Thank you, Aunt Nikki."

Nikki smiled wide at Alex and then handed the next bag to her own child.

"Mine!" TJ cried out one more time.

"Say please," Travis ordered, looking down at our son as sternly as a father could when he thought his kid was cute, but he was trying to teach him manners.

Being a parent was tough sometimes.

"Why are we going to the lake?" I asked the room.

"Apparently our parents were miffed that y'all did a courthouse wedding and then refused to have a reception. So now they're going to use this lovely Memorial Day weekend as an excuse for everyone to get together and bring y'all presents."

"But we don't need presents," I tried.

"Too bad for you," Michael shoved a donut into my face.

I took it from him before he could shove the chocolate too far up my nose, and then licked my lips.

"But…"

"No buts!"

I sighed and took a seat at the island.

"So, when are we going to the lake?"

***

Travis

Six and a half hours later

"Has she applied at the clinic again?"

I looked over to Michael.

"Nope." I shook my head. "She said she's not doing the clinic again, even though they need money and more staff. When she started working for me when I was in the hospital, she kind of took over. I've never gotten her to leave again."

"You don't want her to leave," Baylor said, butting into my conversation.

I shrugged. "He's right, I don't."

Michael smiled.

"Wolf's here."

I looked over to find Wolf, his wife Raven, and his kids running around at his side.

"Imagine that."

Wolf looked up when I said that and headed over.

"Travis."

I offered Wolf my hand and said, "Wolf."

We still weren't the greatest of friends, but I would forever be grateful for the role he played when it came to my wife when we both needed him the most.

"How's it going?"

Wolf grinned at Michael.

"I got some interesting news today."

"Oh, yeah?" I asked. "What kind of news?"

"You remember the agent in Hannah's case?" he asked.

I nodded.

"Apparently he accidentally killed some guy that was involved in a school shooting in Ohio. Lost his job with the FBI."

My brows rose at that.

"Yeah?"

Wolf's smile was fierce. "Yep. Heard he's looking."

I snorted.

"I could always use someone at the club or the shop," I said. "But I doubt a guy like him would like to get his hands dirty."

Wolf's smile was a little weird.

"I don't know much about Parker, but he's got a reputation. He was also once a SEAL. I have a feeling that he's used to getting his hands dirty."

I grunted. "Send him on over, then."

"I'm not sure Parker is a man that will be 'sent over,'" he said. "But I'll pass on the offer."

"You do that."

"He did ask how she was doing."

My brows rose.

"No shit?"

Wolf nodded. "Got a little more info on him, too."

"What kind of info?" I reached for my beer that was sitting on the bow of the boat that was pulled up onto the grass.

"The kind of info that tells me why he is the way he is."

"You already told us why he was so gung-ho," Michael put in.

Wolf grunted something under his breath.

"Yeah, but what you didn't know was that the kid that died in that school shooting wasn't really his kid. It was this kid he did a big brother thing for. It's the kind of program where you try to mentor underprivileged children. Try to keep them on the right path."

I nodded my head.

"Yeah, and?"

"And, I heard from another motorcycle club that Parker was in a gang in his youth, and slit someone's neck as a gang initiation."

My mouth fell open.

"No shit?"

"No shit," Wolf confirmed.

"What are y'all talking about?"

I looped my arm around Hannah's shoulders and brought her to my chest, dropping a kiss to her forehead.

My wife.

Damn, but it still felt odd calling her that after all this time.

"Wolf was telling me that the agent that was investigating the case with Allegra at the school is looking for work, and might come down here."

Hannah's eyes widened.

"He's not with the FBI anymore?"

I shook my head. "Apparently not."

TJ chose that moment to come streaking by, his bare ass startling white, as Alex and Reggie chased behind him.

"I wonder where he got the naked gene from?" Michael teased.

Hannah flipped him off. "I was not naked like that."

Michael walked away while bursting out laughing.

Wolf followed moments later when his wife called his name from across the campground where every single campsite had been rented by my parents for the entire weekend.

"How's it going, sweetheart?"

She threw her hands around my chest and buried her face in between my pecs.

Her hand played along the dotting of scars.

"I wanted to tell you that I got a call."

"Okay," I said. "What did this call say?"

"It was Tate. He was calling to tell you that one of the trucks broke down…and that Dante came into the office today."

My eyes went up at that.

"No shit?"

She shook her head. "No shit." She paused. "He stayed for about twenty minutes, and left with a bag of something."

Worry rolled through me.

"Damn."

She nodded in sympathy. "Might be time to call him again."

I knew that.

It'd been almost two and a half years now since he'd lost his family, and not a day went by that I didn't think about him.

Wonder how the hell he was doing, or where he was.

I sighed and tightened my arms around her, then dropped my mouth to her head.

"We'll worry about what he came to get when we get home," I said. "In the meantime, we're going to act like there's nothing else wrong."

She snorted.

"Like the fact that your brother is in town, and that I also got told by Wolf that he checked into how Allegra was doing at her new prison, and they said she'd been in solitary confinement for a month?"

I shrugged.

A year ago, almost exactly, Allegra had been sentenced to fifteen years in jail. Nine months ago, she was moved to a women's penitentiary in Huntsville, Texas. From there, I'd only heard bad things, and all of them pertained to Allegra's awful mouth, and how she was lucky she wasn't shivved on a daily basis.

It wasn't often that I heard anything about her, but knowing that she wasn't having an easy go of it made me feel all warm and fuzzy inside.

I didn't want her to die, per se, but I also wouldn't complain if someone ate all the good food off her plate every day, either.

Ultimately, everything had worked out.

Hannah had kept her nursing license, as well as her concealed carry license. My kids were healthy and safe. Allegra was not only permanently out of the picture, but she was suffering.

But I always felt like I was waiting for the other shoe to drop.

Like something more was going to happen.

And honestly, maybe something would.

But I needed to realize that I couldn't control everything. That something may happen, but with the woman currently in my arms by my side, I could overcome just about fucking anything.

"Why the serious face, Trav?"

I looked to her face, and smiled. "I'm thinking about what I would do without you."

She frowned.

"Don't you know?"

"Don't I know what?" I asked.

"That you'll never have to know."

I smiled down at her.

"Is that right?"

She nodded once. "Damn right."

I hugged her to me and buried my face into her neck.

While the sound of our family and friends surrounded us, I thanked my lucky stars that I had this newfound happiness.

How'd I get so fucking lucky?

ABOUT THE AUTHOR

Lani Lynn Vale is married to the love of her life that she met in high school. She fell in love with him because he was wearing baseball pants. Ten years later they have three perfectly crazy children and a cat named Demon who likes to wake her up at ungodly times in the night. They live in the greatest state in the world, Texas. She writes contemporary and romantic suspense, and has a love for all things romance. You can find Lani in front of her computer writing away in her fictional characters' world...that is until her husband and kids demand sustenance in the form of food and drink.

Made in the USA
San Bernardino, CA
05 July 2020

74878676R00168